William Elsey Connelley

Wyandot Folk-lore

William Elsey Connelley

Wyandot Folk-lore

ISBN/EAN: 9783744767149

Printed in Europe, USA, Canada, Australia, Japan

Cover: Foto ©Andreas Hilbeck / pixelio.de

More available books at **www.hansebooks.com**

THE CRANE CLASSICS

WYANDOT
FOLK-LORE

THE CRANE CLASSICS

THE CRANE CLASSICS furnish reading matter of a high order for Teachers, Reading Circles, advanced class work, and for select general reading. Numbers published are as follows:

Crane & Company, Publishers, Topeka

*THE TWENTIETH CENTURY CLASSICS
AND SCHOOL READINGS*

UNDER THE EDITORIAL SUPERVISION OF

W. M. DAVIDSON

SUPERINTENDENT OF THE PUBLIC SCHOOLS OF TOPEKA, KANSAS

WYANDOT FOLK-LORE

WYANDOT FOLK-LORE

BY

WILLIAM ELSEY CONNELLEY

Author of "The Provisional Government of Nebraska Territory," "James Henry Lane,
The 'Grim Chieftain' of Kansas," "The Folk-Lore of the Wyandots," etc., etc.

"So the day of their glory is over,
And out on the desolate waste
The far-scattered remnants yet hover,
Like shades of the long-vanished past."

CRANE & COMPANY, PUBLISHERS
TOPEKA, KANSAS
1899

Lo, the poor Indian, whose untutored mind
Sees God in clouds or hears him in the wind;
His soul proud Science never taught to stray
Far as the solar walk, or Milky Way;
Yet simpler Nature to his hope has given,
Behind the cloud-topped hill, an humbler heaven;
Some safer world, in depth of wood embraced,
Some happier island in the watery waste,
Where slaves once more their native land behold,
No friends torment, no Christians thirst for gold.
To be, contents his natural desire;
He asks no angel's wing, no seraph's fire;
But thinks, admitted to that equal sky,
His faithful dog shall bear him company.

—Pope.

I STAND by our Grandmother in the great Yooh-wah-tah-yoh in the North. She speaks to me of the land of the Little People. She directs us to that land. She says to me, "My son, take this torch of fire. It is made from the brand given by your Grandfather. It is a guide in the darkness — a weapon powerful by the way. These it shall be to you as you journey to that land. And I shall come when all my children are there."

I take the torch. The darkness rolls away. I see afar the land of the Little People. It is the land of our Mother, the Turtle. I come into the land of strange light. The waters are blue as the sky; they sparkle and glitter in the light. They are sweet, and the deer delights to drink them as they tumble among the stones. The rivers run towards the South. At the foot of the tall rock the great stream rolls. The swaying bushes are thick upon its shores. They bend to the breezes of that land. Trees are where I stand, upon a crag which rises from the flat mountain-top. The river is under my feet. A warrior comes to me. He says:

"There is one more trial of your courage. Look beyond the river. There lies the land of the Little People."

Then I looked. There was the bright sunshine on the groves and fields. The land rose in swells. It rolled in gentle hills. Great beams of light shone more strongly at some points. The hills were beautiful. The Little People were there. And a great host stood upon the mountains. They were the Wyandots of old. Then did my courage burn strong within me. Then did I say —.
—[*Fragment of an old Wyandot song.*

PREFATORY NOTES

The folk-lore of the Wyandots should be peculiarly interesting to Kansas students. It will be conceded, I believe, that the emigrant tribes were in every way superior to the native tribes of Kansas Indians. The Wyandots were the recognized head of the emigrant tribes. And this superiority had been accorded them by the emigrant tribes themselves. It was of ancient date and long standing. As early as 1750 the Northwestern Confederacy was formed, and the Wyandots were made the keepers of the council-fire thereof. In 1848 this Confederacy was renewed in Kansas at a great council held near Fort Leavenworth, and the Wyandots confirmed in their ancient and honorable position.

As a tribe the Wyandots favored the organization of Nebraska (Kansas) Territory. Indeed, they made the first effective efforts in this direction. They established a Provisional government at the mouth of the Kansas river, in 1853. The first man to bear the title of Governor of Nebraska (Kansas) was William Walker, a Wyandot Indian, a gentleman of education, refinement, and great strength of character. The metropolis of the

(7)

State is but the development of a Wyandot village into a great modern city.

Twenty years ago, seeing that no collection of the folk-lore of this interesting people had ever been attempted, I began to gather and record such of it as I could find. Most of it had then been lost by the tribe. This will not seem strange when it is known that Wyandots were even at that time of more than one-half white blood. There is not so much as a half-blood Wyandot now living. The last full-blood Wyandot died in Canada about 1820. I began the work at a most fortunate time. There were then living many very old Wyandots who remembered much of their tribal history and folk-lore. These are now dead, with but a single exception. The generation now living could furnish no folk-lore of value. Few of them speak their language. Not half a dozen of them can speak the pure Wyandot. Their reservation near Seneca, Missouri, in the Indian Territory, is not different from the well-tilled portions of our country. They are good farmers, and have schools and churches. Stĭh-yĕh'-stäh, or Captain Bull-Head, was the last pagan Wyandot; he died in Wyandotte county, Kansas, about the year 1860.

In the *Journal of American Folk-Lore* for June, 1899, I published a paper on the " Folk-Lore of the Wyandots." The following explanatory note of my work will be found on page 125; it tells how I came to begin this work:

"The writer of this paper, author of the *Provisional Government of Nebraska Territory*, member of the Nebraska State Historical

Society, and chairman of the Committee on American Ethnology, Western Historical Society, Kansas City, Mo., is an adopted Wyandot of the Deer Clan, raised up to fill the position of Sahr′-stahr-rah′-tseh, the famous chief of the Wyandots known to history as the Half-King. The latter was chief during the war of the Revolution, and one of the founders of the Northwestern Confederacy of Indians, that opposed so long the settlement of the territory northwest of the Ohio river. The Wyandots stood at the head of this confederacy, and were the keepers of the Council Fire thereof.

" The writer, who has also received the Wyandot name of Deh′-hehn-yahn′-teh, The Rainbow, has had frequent occasion to transact business for this people, and in the course of such duty has become interested in their language, history, manners, customs, and religious beliefs. He has also written an account of the clan system and other features of the tribal society. He has prepared an extensive vocabulary of the language, not yet published, and made a collection of the songs which by missionaries and others have been rendered into the Wyandot tongue. At the present time the opportunity for such studies has passed away, inasmuch as the old Wyandots from whom this information was received, with one exception, have died, and the present generation is wholly ignorant of the ancient beliefs. No folk-lore could be obtained from any Wyandot now living, and few can speak the language."

Only a brief outline of the folk-lore of the Wyandots can be presented in a work of this kind. And what is given is necessarily divested of much of its force and beauty because of the omission of all Wyandot language in expressing Wyandot terms. Nothing in this field has been published before, and the writer has been encouraged by students in all parts of the country to publish the results of his labors in the interest of science. He has a very extensive Vocabulary of the Wyandot language, the only one ever prepared. It is his intention to publish this and the complete work on the folk-lore of the tribe.

The folk-lore of the Wyandots contains many beautiful things. It is to be hoped that our teachers will come to see the beauties of all American folk-lore, and give it that attention which it deserves from American students. It is practically an unexplored field. Treasures lie hidden in it. Who will lend a hand to dig them out?

WM. E. C.

TOPEKA, KANSAS, November 11, 1899.

HISTORICAL REVIEW

GENERAL REMARKS

But all the story of the night told over,
And all their minds transfigur'd so together,
More witnesseth than fancy's images,
And grows to something of great constancy,
But, howsoever, strange and admirable.
—*A Midsummer Night's Dream.*

The term "folk-lore" is broad in its significance; it embraces much. The traditional customs and beliefs of a people are a part of their folk-lore. This may apply to those believed in or practiced in the present; it has special application to those of a past age. Traditions handed down from father to son are a part of the folk-lore of a people. Where isolation or ignorance gives rise to superstitious tales and beliefs, we include these in the folk-lore of that people. It does not always follow that a custom or a saying must be of a long-gone age, to become a part of our folk-lore. The folk-lore of our own times is enriched by many of the quaint and homely sayings of Franklin. Beliefs and superstitions of ages long gone by, or so remote in origin that they are attributed to a divine origin, belong to folk-lore. We now make this term include what is properly mythology. Of the two terms, "folk-lore" and "mythology," folk-lore is by far the

(11)

most comprehensive in its modern acceptation. It follows that a belief need not embrace a truth to become folk-lore. Most folk-lore is made up of scientific absurdities. All mythology consists of ancient beliefs now demonstrated to be incorrect and erroneous.

This last proposition being true, where is the profit in the study of the folk-lore and mythology of a people? The answer and reason lie in the fact that the folk-lore is the record of the progress of a people. Their ancient beliefs lie embodied in it. If we can find out what a people have believed in a bygone age, we can from that determine the condition of such people in that age. All development, animate and inanimate, has been the same. We examine the rocks of a certain age of the earth, and ascertain precisely the conditions of the earth at that time. For only certain well-known, well-defined, and scientifically demonstrated physical conditions can produce such results as we find existing in such age. Folk-lore might well be denominated the geology of the progress of the human mind. For certain degrees of development of the human mind produce certain thoughts and actions which are impossible to any other degree of its advancement. Folk-lore thus become in a sense the record of human progress, but more particularly the record of the development of the mind from savagery to civilization. As an instance simple and easily comprehended, we cite the homely adage, "A bird in the hand is worth two in the bush." Only a people of a practical turn could have originated it. But how many centuries passed with the principle recognized but without any concise expression of it! This is the simplest form in which this truth can be expressed; the whole subject is crystallized, and its form becomes a proverb. No further progress in simplification can be made; the coinage of this adage marks the close of progress in this particular instance. So it is in all the processes of mental development, both great and small, in all matters, in all times, and in all directions.

Then the emotions of a people during its ages of progress from savagery to civilization are imbedded in its folk-lore. So, also, of the cruelty, tenderness, and all other traits, properties, or qualities of the mind. This is distinctly discernible in the comparison of the folk-lore of one people with that of another—for a contrast, that of the Irish with that of the Corsican; the German with the Arabian, etc. The chief value of folk-lore, though, is in its demonstration of the principle that all human progress has been along certain lines which by it are proved to be inherent in and common to the mind of man. And, further, that all development, of mind and matter, men and worlds, peoples and planetary systems, is along one line here plainly marked for us by the hand of the Infinite.

American folk-lore is the result of the foregoing principles applied to the Indians, the aboriginal inhabitants of our country. For the white race in America have not become a people with a distinct folk-lore. We are yet developing the Gaelic, Saxon, German and other folk-lores. So the term "American folk-lore" as yet applies only to that of the aborigines.

We find in the North-American Indians many distinct families and all degrees of mental strength. The folk-lore preserved indicates that this has always been true.

Where we find the figures bold, clear, well defined, stamped with strong characteristics, we say that the people originating it were brave, hardy, mentally strong, and possessed of well-defined objects, aims and tendencies which they were consciously or unconsciously developing. If, on the other hand, we find a tribal folk-lore confused, with no well-defined characters or figures, but with only dim and indistinct outlines, we say at once that the people producing it were low mentally, of an inferior type, possessing no vigor of mind. The folk-lore of the Iroquoian family of Indians is one of the strongest, boldest, most striking found in America. And there is little doubt but that of the Wyandots is the foremost in these features found in the folk-lores of the Iroquoian family. In boldness, originality, clearness of perception and strength of conception the folk-lore of the Wyandots surpasses that of any other tribe with which I am familiar.

We repeat, that in all the lands of the earth man has advanced from savagery towards civilization along the same general lines. The bone awl, the thread of sinew, the skin garment, the shell ornament, the stone implement, the bow and the arrow, are not peculiar to the people of the New World. And this fact makes the study of primitive man as found in the forests of North America one of supreme importance—of intense interest. For here we may see ways similar in many respects to those which the Semite, the Egyptian, the Greek, the Celt, the Teuton trod in their ever restless, irresistible, often unconscious and unconsenting advancement to something higher and better.

In the following pages I have endeavored to set out

truthfully the degree of mental attainment, the condition and character of the social, political and religious institutions of the ancient Wyandots as evidenced by the fragments of their legendary lore that have come down to us. Let us look at this people in the pagan days when they had not seen the white man. Let us go back four hundred years and enter the thick woods of Canada and New York. Let us look once again upon the broad, majestic rivers, the clear streams, the boiling rapids, the foaming cataracts, the crystal lakes, all before the paleface had defiled them with his blighting touch. Let us gaze upon the forests, broad, dense, gloomy. We shall hear the winter storm roaring through the branches of the great trees and see the North Wind rend and break them in his wrath. We shall see the thick blanket of snow spread down over the world by Winter. And when spring comes we shall see this scene change within a month. The snows melt, the ice disappears, the North Wind returns to his lair. Leaves spring from every bough; ducks, geese, swans, gulls, pelicans and other water-fowl swim, soar, wade and scream. The silver side of the trout flashes as he leaps above the waters now released from their icy fetters. The wolf prowls, and the panther screams to his fellows. The heavy bear lumbers clumsily through the woods and startles the light and graceful deer. Insects hum and whiz and drone. Spring melts into the full and fruitful summer. The oak, the hickory, the hazel, the beech, the walnut, the wild vine, weight their branches, with fruit to be ripened by the mellow rays of the hazy sun of the voluptuous autumn.

And what of man? He is here. See that village by

the sparkling lake where the blue hills descend gently to the pebbly beach. And another, and still another beyond. Strange people dwell there. They have seen no man different from themselves. Of our arts, our civilization, our religion, they know nothing. Whatever they have of these they have made for themselves. And we shall find that they have an expressive and strong language, strange religious beliefs and complex social systems and political institutions. They cultivate the corn plant, and have domesticated a species of dog. They have become proficient in the cultivation and curing of tobacco, and in the barter of it to surrounding tribes that have come to depend upon them for this Indian luxury and blessing. They long since began to take note of things about them. They have sought to account for all the phenomena of the heavens and the earth.

Their conclusions were fixed by the light they had been able to attain, and are ridiculous when seen in the light we now stand in to view them, but not more so than those of the Chinese, the Greeks, the Celts, the East Indians, the Babylonians, the Assyrians, the Egyptians, and the ancient Teutons. And while they are absurd when measured and weighed by modern science and civilized learning, they are beautiful in conception, and they reveal a mentality of strength and persistency.

I.—NAME.

Lalemant says the original and true name of the Wyandots is OUENDAT.

In history the Wyandots have been spoken of by the following names:

1. Tionnontates,
2. Etionontates,
3. Tuinontatek,
4. Dionondadies,
5. Khionontaterrhonons,
6. Petuneux or Nation du Petun (Tobacco).

They call themselves

1. Wĕhn'-dŭht, or
2. Wĕhn'-dooht.

They never accepted the name *Huron,* which is of French origin. It is not certain that they were entitled to the name *Huron.* They make no such claim themselves.

The Wyandots have been always considered the remnant of the Hurons. That they were related to the people called Hurons by the French, there is no doubt, and upon this point there is no dispute and can be no question. After having studied them carefully for almost twenty

—2 (17)

years, I am of the opinion that the Wyandots are more closely related to the Senecas than they were to the ancient Hurons.

Both myth and tradition of the Wyandots say they were "created" in the region between St. James's Bay and the coast of Labrador. All their traditions describe their ancient home as north of the mouth of the St. Lawrence.

In their traditions of their migrations southward they say they came to the island where Montreal now stands. They took possession of the country along the north bank of the St. Lawrence from the Ottawa river to a large lake and river far below Quebec. The lower or eastern boundary cannot now be definitely fixed. It was bounded by this large river, they say.

This country they called by a name which means, in their language, "the rivers rushing by," or "the country of rushing waters." They claim that while they resided there they numbered many thousands, and that they were the dominant power in all that country.

On the south side of the St. Lawrence lived the Senecas, so the Wyandot traditions recite. The Senecas claimed the island upon which the city of Montreal is built. The Senecas and Wyandots have always claimed a cousin relation with each other. They say that they have been neighbors from time immemorial. Their languages are almost the same, each being the dialect of an older common mother-tongue. They are as nearly alike as are the Seneca and Mohawk dialects. The two tribes live side by side at this time, and each can speak the tongue of the other as well as it speaks its own.

The Wyandots say that the Delawares lived to the east of them, on the lower St. Lawrence, and on its north bank. They were on friendly terms, perhaps in friendly alliance. This part of the tradition I regard as possible, and indeed probable, and proved by the clans or totems of the Delawares, for with them the Turtle Clan is considered the oldest and of most importance. The Delawares are said to be the oldest of Algonquin tribes, and it is more than probable that they obtained their ideas of the importance of the Turtle from the Iroquoian peoples.

To the west of the Wyandot country lived the Ottawas, so the Wyandot traditions claim.

When the Wyandots came to the St. Lawrence, and how long they remained there, cannot now be determined. Their traditions say that they were among those that met Cartier at Hochelaga in 1535. According to their traditions, Hochelaga was a Seneca town.

It has been the opinion of writers upon the subject that the Wyandots migrated from the St. Lawrence directly to the point where they were found by the French. Whatever the fact may be, their traditions tell a different story. They claim to have become involved in a deadly war with the Senecas because of murders committed by a Wyandot at the instigation of a Seneca woman.

· Hale makes Peter D. Clarke say that the Wyandots fled to the northwest to escape the consequences of this war with the Senecas. That they fled for this purpose is true, but neither Clarke nor Wyandot tradition says that they fled to the northwest. Their route was up the St. Lawrence, which they crossed, and along the south shore of Lake Ontario. They held this course until they arrived at the Falls of Niagara, where they settled and remained for some years. They called this point in their wanderings by their name for waterfalls. This Wyandot word means " the stream falls into itself," or " tumbles down to its new level from the rock above." Louisville, Kentucky, was so called by them from the Falls of the Ohio.

The Wyandots removed from the Falls of Niagara, the site now occupied by Toronto, Canada. Their removal from Niagara was in consequence of the Iroquois coming into their historic seat in what is now New York. This settlement they called by their word which means " plenty," or " a land of plenty." They named it so because of the abundance of game and fish they found, and of the abundance of corn, beans, squashes and tobacco they raised. The present name of that city is only a slight change of the old Wyandot name, which was pronounced " To-run-to."

As the Senecas pushed farther westward, the Wyandots became uneasy, and finally abandoned their country at Toronto and migrated northward. Here they came in contact with the Hurons, who tried to expel them, but were unable to do so. The French found them in alliance with the Hurons, but record that they had but recently been at war with that people. When the Jesuits went, among the Hurons the Wyandots were a part of the Huron Confederacy. Their history from this point is well known.

If it turns out that there is any reliance to be placed in the traditions of the Wyandots, they were found in their historic seat about one hundred and five years from the time they were first seen by the French at Montreal in 1535. Their migration from the St. Lawrence, by way of the Niagara Falls and Toronto to the Blue Mountains on the shores of the Nottawassaga Bay, occurred after the French first came to Canada.

The Wyandots were involved in the general ruin wrought by the Iroquois. I subjoin a short account by Parkman of the wanderings of the Wyandots after the destruction of the Hurons by the Five Nations. It is taken from "The Jesuits in North America," which should be read by every one desiring a knowledge of the Wyandots at all full or complete:

" In the woody valleys of the Blue Mountains, south of the Nottawassaga Bay of Lake Huron, and two days' journey west of the frontier Huron towns, lay the nine villages of the Tobacco Nation, or Tionnontates. In manners as in language, they closely resembled the Hurons. Of old they were their enemies, but were now at peace with them, and about the year 1640 became their close confederates. Indeed, in the ruin which befell that hapless people, the Tionnontates alone retained a tribal organization; and their descendants, with a trifling exception, are to this day the sole inheritors of the Huron or Wyandot name. Expatriated and wandering, they held for generations a paramount influence among the Western tribes. In their original seats among the Blue Mountains, they offered an example extremely rare among Indians, of a tribe raising a crop for the market; for they traded in tobacco largely with other tribes. Their Huron confederates, keen traders, would not suffer them to pass through their country to traffic with the French, preferring to secure for themselves the advantage of bartering with them in French goods at an enormous profit.

" The division of the Hurons called the Tobacco Nation, favored by their isolated position among the mountains, held their ground longer than the rest; but at length they, too, were compelled to fly, together with such other Hurons as had taken refuge with them. They made their way northward, and settled on the Island of Michilimackinac, where they were joined by the Ottawas, who with other Algonquins had been driven by fear of the Iroquois from the western shores of Lake Huron and the banks of the River Ottawa. At Michilimackinac the Hurons and their allies were again attacked by the Iroquois, and, after remaining several years, they made another move, and took possession of the islands at the mouth of the Green Bay of Lake Michigan. Even here their old enemy did not leave them in peace; whereupon they fortified themselves on the mainland, and afterwards migrated southward and westward. This brought them in contact with the Illinois, an Algonquin people, at that time very numerous, but who, like many other tribes at this epoch, were doomed to a rapid diminution from wars with other savage nations. Continuing their migration westward, the Hurons and Ottawas reached the Mississippi, where they fell in with the Sioux. They soon quarreled with those fierce children of the prairie, who drove them from their country. They retreated to the southwestern extremity of Lake Superior, and settled on Point Saint Esprit, or Shagwamigon Point, near the Islands of the Twelve Apostles. As the Sioux continued to harass them, they left this place about the year 1671, and

returned to Michilimackinac, where they settled, not on
the island, but on the neighboring point, St. Ignace, now
Graham's Point, on the north side of the strait. The
greater part of them afterwards removed thence to Detroit and Sandusky, where they lived under the name of
Wyandots until the present century, maintaining a marked
influence over the surrounding Algonquins. They bore
an active part, on the side of the French, in the war which
ended in the reduction of Canada; and they were the
most formidable enemies of the English in the Indian
war under Pontiac. The government of the United
States at length removed them to reserves on the Western
frontier, where a remnant of them may still be found.
Thus it appears that the Wyandots, whose name is so con-
spicuous in the history of our border wars, are descendants
of the ancient Hurons, and chiefly of that portion of them
called the Tobacco Nation."

The Wyandots came to what is now Wyandotte county,
Kansas, in the summer and fall of 1843, from Wyandot
county, Ohio. They had been promised 148,000 acres
of land in Kansas, but so large a body could not then be
found unclaimed. They turned to their old friends, their
nephews, the Delawares, who had been removed West some
years before and given a large reservation on the north
side of the Kansas river, the eastern boundary of which
was the Missouri river. The Delawares sold them the land
in the fork of the Missouri and Kansas rivers. Their
reservation consisted of thirty-nine sections of land, for
which they paid the Delawares $48,000. This land is
all in Wyandotte county.

Most of the Wyandots were civilized when they arrived in Kansas. But there were pagans among them to the number of about one hundred. They brought with them a Methodist Church fully organized, to which some two hundred and fifty of them belonged. This was the old mission founded at Upper Sandusky by John Stewart and James B. Finley, and was the first mission ever established by the Methodist Episcopal Church. It is now the Washington Avenue M. E. Church, in Kansas City, Kansas.

In 1855 the Wyandots made a treaty in which they dissolved their tribal relations and received their land in severalty, and became citizens of the United States. In 1867 the Government allowed such of them as desired to do so to resume their tribal relations, and purchased them a reservation of twenty thousand acres from the Senecas, in the Indian Territory. This reservation is near Seneca, Mo., and the Wyandot tribe live on it at the present time. This land is allotted to them, and is in a good state of cultivation, they being good farmers, and an industrious and orderly people. They maintain schools for their children, and many of them are members of the churches of the Methodist and Quaker denominations. They have good dwellings; and much stock, consisting of hogs, cattle and horses, is raised and sold. The thriving little town of Wyandotte, on the Frisco railroad, is the metropolis of their country. It is situated in one of the most beautiful valleys in the Indian Territory.

The Wyandots are now more white than Indian. They are a generous and hospitable people, and very kind and obliging to strangers.

II.—WYANDOT GOVERNMENT.

The government of the ancient Wyandots was, in its highest functions, a pure democracy. While it rested upon the system of *clans*[1] for the execution of its details, anything affecting the interests of the whole people was decided in a mass convention convened according to well-defined custom or law. In this convention women had as much voice as the men.

The tribe was anciently divided into twelve clans, or gentes. Each of these had a local government, consisting of a clan counsel presided over by a clan chief. These clan counsels were composed of at least five persons, one man and four women, and they might contain any number of women above four. Any business pertaining purely to the internal affairs of the clans was carried to the clan councils for settlement. An appeal was allowed from the clan council to the tribal council. The four women of the clan council regulated the clan affairs and selected the clan chief. The office of clan chief was in a measure hereditary, although not wholly so. The tribal council was composed of the clan chiefs, the hereditary sachem, and such other men of the tribe of renown as the sachem might with the consent of the tribal council call to the council-fire. In determining a question the vote was by clans, and not by individuals. In matters of great importance it required a unanimous vote to carry a proposition.

---

[1] Gens is a better word—the proper word. But the Wyandots say *clan* or tribe when speaking of this tribal subdivision.

The names of the ancient clans of the Wyandot tribe are as follows:

1. Big Turtle.
2. Little Turtle.
3. Mud Turtle.
4. Wolf.
5. Bear.
6. Beaver.
7. Deer.
8. Porcupine.
9. Striped Turtle.
10. Highland Turtle, or Prairie Turtle.
11. Snake.
12. Hawk.

These clan names are all expressed in Wyandot words so long and hard to properly pronounce that they are omitted here. They are written in what the Wyandots call the Order of Precedence and Encampment, as I have recorded them above. On the march the warriors of the Big Turtle Clan marched in front, those of the Little Turtle Clan marched next to them, and so on down to the last clan, except the Wolf Clan, which had command of the march and might be where its presence was most necessary. The tribal encampment was formed " on the shell of the Big Turtle," as the old Wyandots said. This means that the tents were arranged in a circular form as though surrounding the shell of the Big Turtle. The Big Turtle Clan was placed where the right fore-leg of the turtle was supposed to be and the other clans were arranged around in their proper order, except the Wolf Clan, which could be in the center of the inclosure on the turtle's back, or in front of it where the turtle's head was supposed to be, as it was thought best. In ancient times all their villages were built in this order, and in the tribal council the clans took this order in seating themselves, with the sachem either in the center or in the front of the circle, and the chief of the Wolf Clan attending at the door of the council chamber.

These clans were separated into two divisions, called phratries. The first phratry consisted of the following tribes:

1. Bear.
2. Deer.
3. Snake.
4. Hawk.

The second phratry consisted of the following tribes:

1. Big Turtle.
2. Little Turtle.
3. Mud Turtle.
4. Beaver.
5. Porcupine.
6. Striped Turtle.
7. Highland Turtle, or Prairie Turtle.

The Mediator, Executive Power, and Umpire of the tribe was the Wolf Clan, which stood between the phratries, and bore a cousin relation to each.

All the clans of a phratry bore the relation of brothers to one another, and the clans of one phratry bore the relation of cousins to those of the other phratry.

Their marriage laws were fixed by this relationship.

Anciently a man of the first phratry was compelled to marry a woman of the second phratry, and *vice versa*. This was because every man of a phratry was supposed to be the brother of every other man in it, and every woman in the phratry was supposed to be his sister. The law of marriage is now so modified that it applies only to the clans, a man of the Deer Clan being permitted to marry a woman of Bear, Snake, Hawk, or any other clan but his own. Indeed, even this modification has now almost disappeared. If a man of the Deer Clan married a woman of the Porcupine Clan, all his children were of the Porcupine Clan, for the gens always follows the woman and never the man. The descent and distribution of property followed the same law; the son could inherit nothing from his father, for they were always of different clans. A man's property descended to his nearest kindred through his mother. The woman is always the head of the Wyandot family.

Five of the ancient clans of the Wyandots are extinct. They are as follows: (1) Mud Turtle; (2) Beaver; (3) Striped Turtle; (4) Highland, or Prairie Turtle; (5) Hawk.

Those still in existence are as follows: (1) Big Turtle; (2) Little Turtle; (3) Wolf; (4) Deer; (5) Bear; (6) Porcupine; (7) Snake.

The present government of the Wyandot tribe is based on this ancient division of the tribes. An extract from the Constitution may be of interest. It was adopted September 23, 1873:

"It shall be the duty of the said Nation to elect their

officers on the second Tuesday in July of each year.
That said election shall be conducted in the following
manner. Each Tribe (clan), consisting of the following
Tribes: The Big and Little Turtle, Porcupine, Deer,
Bear, and Snake, shall elect a chief; and then the Big
and Little Turtle and Porcupine Tribes shall select one of
their three chiefs as a candidate for Principal Chief. The
Deer, Bear, and Snake Tribes shall also select one of their
three Chiefs as a candidate for Principal Chief; and then
at the general election to be held on the day above mentioned, the one receiving the highest number of votes cast
shall be declared the Principal Chief; the other shall be
declared the Second Chief. The above-named Tribes shall
on the above-named election day elect one or more sheriffs.

" The Wolf Tribe shall have the right to elect a Chief
whose duty shall be that of Mediator.

" In case of misdemeanor on the part of any Chief,
for the first offense the Council shall send the Mediator to
warn the party; for the second offense the party offending
shall be liable to removal by the Mediator, or Wolf and
his Clan, from office."

This has always been the position and office of the
Wolf Clan.

Anciently the office of sachem or head chief was in a
manner hereditary in a clan and in a family, but if the
heir was considered unfit to exercise authority he was
passed over, and a sachem selected by the tribal council.
In this event the chief was first nominated by the chiefs
of the Big Turtle, Deer, and Bear Clans, but not neces-

sarily from their own clans, and never from the Bear
Clan. The nomination was from the family of the chief
passed over unless there was no suitable person in the
family, when it must be from his clan. But in cases of
emergency, or of great ability in a warrior not in the line
of heredity, the hereditary chief, family or clan might be
passed over by the tribal council and the man of superior
ability chosen.

Thus the last Sähr'-stähr-räh'-tseh of the tribe was of
the Deer Clan, and was known to the white men as the
Half King. He was the hereditary sachem of the Wyandots. He died in Detroit in 1788, and was succeeded by
Tarhe of the Porcupine Clan. Tarhe was selected because
of his ability.

The passing over of the candidate entitled to the chieftaincy by heredity did not operate as an entire divestment
of his family or clan of their hereditary rights, and as
soon as they could produce a suitable person for the
office they could demand their rights. After the battle of
Fallen Timbers (with General Wayne), the Deer Clan
was permanently divested of its hereditary right, the
sachemship. This was done at the instance of the Porcupine Clan, which had possessed the chieftaincy since the
death of the Half King, but the Deer Clan protested
against this infringement of the ancient law, and its
hereditary right, and has never relinquished claim to
the hereditary right to select the sachem.

The office of Sähr'-stähr-räh'-tseh was a special creation,
and the highest conferred by the tribe. This officer was
in power like our President, and like our General of the
army, and like the Pope, possessing the highest political,

military and spiritual power. It was not often bestowed.
After the death of the Half King it remained vacant
until the present writer was "raised up" to fill his place,
on the 22d day of March, 1899.

The origin of these clans is hidden in the obscurity of
great antiquity. They are of religious origin. We learn
something of them from the Wyandot mythology, or
folk-lore. The ancient Wyandots believed that they were
descended from these-animals, for whom their clans were
named. The animals from which they were descended
were different from the animal of the same species to-
day. They were deities, zoölogical gods. The animals
of the same species are descended from them. These
Animals were the creators of the universe. The Big
Turtle made the Great Island, as North America was
called by the Wyandots, and he bears it on his back to
this day. The Little Turtle made the sun, moon, and
many of the stars. The Mud Turtle made a hole through
the Great Island for the sun to pass back to the East
through after setting at night, so he could rise upon a
new day. While making this hole through the Great Isl-
and the Mud Turtle turned aside from her work long
enough to fashion the future home of the Wyandots, their
happy hunting-grounds, to which they go after death.
The sun shines there at night while on his way back to the
East. This land is called the land of the Little People, a
race of pigmies created to assist the Wyandots. They
live in it, and preserve the ancient customs, habits, beliefs, language and government of the Wyandots for their
use after they leave this world by death. These Little

People come and go through the "living rock," but the Wyandots must go to it by way of a great underground city where they were once hidden while the works of the world were being restored after destruction in a war between two brothers who were gods.

I only stop a moment to note the fact that the ancient belief of the Hindoos pictured the world as borne up by a great turtle. Is it not entirely possible that it may be determined that America is the cradle of the human race, and that Asia was peopled from America? The Indian belongs to the Mongolian race, and there are many traits common to them and the Chinese. It is possible that when we study the Indians we study the oldest people in the world, instead of the youngest.

The religion of the Wyandots was undergoing slow change when arrested by the coming of the white man. The old Animal-gods were slowly giving place to two brothers born of a woman who fell down from heaven. One of these was good and the other bad. We shall learn of them in the mythology.

All Wyandot proper names had their foundation in this clan system. They were clan names. The unit of the Wyandot social and political systems was not the family nor the individual, but the clan. The child belonged to its clan first, to its parents afterwards. Each clan had its list of proper names, and this list was its exclusive property which no other clan could appropriate or use. They were necessarily clan names. They were constructed according to rigid rules and usages prescribed by immemorial custom, and the laws of the Medes and Persians were more easily changed than those of the ancient

Tionnontates. No laws of nations are so rigidly enforced
as was custom in Indian tribes in ancient times. Custom
was inflexible—exacting—and could be modified only by
long and persistent effort (and then by almost impercep-
tible degrees), or by national disaster.

The customs and usages governing the formation of
clan proper names demanded that they be derived from
some part, habit, action or peculiarity of the animal from
which the clan was supposed to be descended. Or they
might be derived from some property, law, or peculiarity
of the element in which such animal lived. Thus a proper
name was always a distinctive badge of the clan bestow-
ing it.

When death left unused any original clan proper name,
the next child born into the clan, if of the sex to which the
vacant name belonged, had such vacated name bestowed
upon it. If no child was born, and a stranger was
adopted, this name was given to such adopted person.
This was the unchangeable law, and there was but one
proviso or exception to it. When a child was born under
some extraordinary circumstance, or peculiarity, or with
some distinguishing mark, or a stranger adopted with
these, the council-women of the clan informed themselves
of all the facts and devised a name in which all these
facts were imbedded. This name was made to conform
to the ancient law governing clan proper names if possible, but often this could not be done. These special names
died with their owners, and were never perpetuated.

The parents were not permitted to name the child; the
clan bestowed the name. Names were given but once a

—3

year, and always at the ancient anniversary of the Green
Corn Feast. Anciently, formal adoptions could be made
at no other time. The name was bestowed by the clan
chief. He was a civil officer of both his clan and the
tribe. At an appointed time in the ceremonies of the
Green Corn Feast each clan chief took an assigned position, which in ancient times was the Order of Precedence
and Encampment, and parents having children to be
named filed before him in the order of the ages of the
children to be named. The council-women stood by the
clan chief, and announced to him the name of each child
presented, for all clan proper names were made by the
council-women. The chief then bestowed the name upon
the child. This he could do by simply announcing the
name to the parents, or by taking the child in his arms
and addressing it by the name selected for it.

The adoption of a stranger was into some family by
consent, or at the instance of the principal woman of the
family. It was not necessary that the adoption be made
at the Green Corn Feast. The adoption was not considered complete, however, until it was ratified by the clan
chief at the Green Corn Feast. This ratification might
be accomplished in the simple ceremonial of being presented at this time to the clan chief by one of the Sheriffs.
His clan name was bestowed upon him, and he was wel-
comed in a few well-chosen words, and the ceremony was
complete. Or the adoption might be performed with as
much display, ceremony and pomp as the tribal council
might, from any cause, decree. The tribal council con-
trolled in some degree the matter of adoptions. In ancient times, when many prisoners of war were brought in

it determined how many should be tortured and how many adopted.

A man (and perhaps a woman) might have two names, sometimes more. He was not prohibited from assuming an additional name. The tribal council might order a special name bestowed upon him for distinguished services to the nation. But these were only incidental names, and he might be called by them or not as his fellows chose. His clan name was his true name, and while he might have others, he could not repudiate it nor lay it aside. Whatever he was to his tribe, or to others, he was to his clan only what his clan name indicated, and he was almost always so called. Any additional names he might possess died with him; they were never perpetuated.

This manner of naming was advantageous. A man disclosed his clan in telling his name. The clan was his mother; he was the child of the clan; his name was his badge and always a sure means of identification.

I give a few Wyandot clan proper names. They illustrate the principles involved in naming.

1. GEORGE WRIGHT.—Wolf Clan. Häh-shēh'-träh. Means the footprints of the wolf.

2. ALFRED MUDEATER.—Porcupine Clan. Rēh-hōōh'-zhäh. Means the act of the porcupine in pulling down the branches and nipping off the buds and bark.

3. MRS. ALFRED MUDEATER.—Deer Clan. Mĕhn'-dĭh-dĕh'-tĭh. Means the echo; the wonderful talker; what she says goes a long way and then comes back again. Refers to the deer's voice echoing in the night when calling to his fellows.

4. ROBERT ROBITAILLE.—Bear Clan. Tĕh-hōōh'-käh-

quäh'-shrōōh. Means " Bear with four eyes." So named because he wore spectacles when he was adopted.

5. CHARLES LOFLAND.—Snake Clan. Tĕh'-hōōh-mäh'-yĕhs. Means " You cannot see him," or " He is invisible."

6. MRS. SARAH DAGNETT.— Snake Clan. Has two names. First, Yäh'-äh-täh'-sĕh. Means "a new body"; said of a snake when it slips off its old skin, as a snake does at least once every year. Second, Ooh'-däh-tōhn'-tĕh. Means " She has left her village." One of the first (if not the very first) names in the list of names for women belonging to the Snake Clan. See my " Origin of the Snake Clan " for the origin and full meaning of this name.

7. WILLIAM WALKER.—Big Turtle Clan. He was Provisional Governor of Nebraska (Kansas) Territory. Had two names. First, Sēhs'-täh-rōh. Means " bright," and refers to the turtle's eye shining in the water. Second, Häh-shäh'-rēhs. Means " overfull," and refers to a stream overflowing its banks at flood.

8. MRS. CATHERINE JOHNSON.— Deer Clan. Yäh-rōhn'-yäh-äh-wĭh. Means " The deer goes into the sky and everywhere."

9. ALLEN JOHNSON, JR.—Deer Clan. Shrīh'-äh-wähs. Means " Cannot find deer when he goes hunting."

The Wyandot supposed that to increase the size of the clan to which he belonged he would please the Animal-god from which it was descended. He made every effort to keep his clan full; that is, keep the full list of names belonging to it all in use. For this purpose he made war to secure women and children for adoption; warriors were often captured for adoption. The old Wyandots have often told me that their tribe made war on the Cherokees for the express purpose of securing women and children with which to make good the wasting clans. To allow a clan to become extinct was sure to call down the displeasure of the Animal-god for which the clan was named and from which it was supposed it was descended. But notwithstanding these incentives to keep the clans alive, two of them were extinct as much as a century ago, if not before that time. Others became extinct about the time of the removal to Kansas. The majority of the tribe were then civilized and Christianized, and the pagan interest in such matters waned and received less attention.

III.—RELIGION.

The gods of the Wyandots were those of the Iroquois and the Hurons, but they were stamped with a strong Wyandot individuality, and in many respects differed in attributes from those of the nations named. The Wyandot was more Iroquois than he was Huron-Iroquois, and he was but little different from the Seneca. It need surprise no one if it is finally determined that the Wyandots were the oldest of the Iroquoian family. Their mythology makes clear some things left in uncertainty and obscurity by that of other tribes of the family. There are some things in it that are not found in the myths of any of the other tribes. Their myths, too, are clearer cut, more definite, and, I believe, more beautiful in form, than those of other tribes. The Iroquoian family has been supposed to possess little imagination, and a mythology deficient in beautiful conceptions. This opinion is the result, I believe, of an imperfect acquaintance with the folk-lore of this strong and bold people. The myths of the woman who fell from heaven, the creation of the great island, the birth of the twins, the enlargement of the great island and the peopling of it with man and animals, the destruction of these and their re-creation, the creation of the sun, moon and stars, and many others, are but little inferior in their bold originality and beauty of conception to the Greek myths.

The Wyandots gave names of their own to the God of the white man, but as it is our intention to omit all Wyandot words as far as possible, these names are not given. The conception of the Great Spirit, which has been attributed to the Indians, was given them by early missionaries. No Indian tribe ever had such a conception until after contact with Europeans. It is certain that no single " Supreme Ruler," or " Creator of the Universe," or of even the world, or any " Manitou " or " Great Spirit " was believed in or conceived of by the ancient Wyandots. This is true also of all the North-American Indians.

They had no conception of a land of punishment after death, to which they went if they were wicked here. Such a conception as the devil of the white man no Indian tribe had until after the missionaries came. They had no word that could be used for swearing oaths. They could not swear in their own language, but soon acquired a choice assortment of profanity from the Christians.

The gods of the ancient Wyandots were those of the Hurons and the Iroquois, but with various differences and modifications in names and attributes. They are stamped with a strong Wyandot individuality, and it need surprise no one if it is finally determined by investigation that the Wyandot conceptions are the originals from which were derived the ideas of the Hurons and other Iroquoian peoples.

The legends and myths of the Wyandots bear a closer conformity to those of the Senecas than they do to those of the Hurons as recorded by the Jesuits, who were the first missionaries to the Huron towns. The traditions of the Wyandots indicate long association with the Senecas, and a comparatively recent separation from them.

But the Wyandots believed there was a world above this, ruled over by a mighty chief. This chief seems to have been immortal. His name might be expressed as the Chief above the sky, or the Mighty Ruler. He ruled the world above the sky, and was the father of the Woman who fell down from heaven. Many supernatural powers were attributed to him. Whether or not the belief in his supernatural powers is the result of a degeneracy of the ancient Wyandot faith from contact with the foreign belief of a stronger people, it may be impossible to satisfactorily determine. But that this belief has existed from time immemorial is the claim of the old Wyandots with whom I have talked upon the subject; and there is nothing to disprove their averment. I may say that it is certain that he was regarded as were Eataentsic and Jouskeha by the Hurons, as recorded by Le June:

" This God and Goddess live like themselves, but without form, make feasts as they do, are lustful as they; in short, they imagine them exactly like themselves. And still, though they make them human and corporal, they seem nevertheless to attribute to them certain immensity in all places."

Even if in the ancient Wyandot mind he always possessed these powers, he did not conform to our idea of
what the Wyandot is supposed to understand or wish to
express by the term " Great Spirit." He ruled only as
the " Head Chief." He had a family; and when any
member of it was sick he called the medicine man, as we
poorly translate the term. In fact, aside from his supposed magical powers, he was there in that land only
what a mighty chief is here in this world. And I have
been able to discover little evidence that he ever interested
himself in the affairs of this lower world or its people.
I have found none at all that he exercised any power or
influence whatever upon the souls of people after their
death and departure from this world. I cannot say that
he was never supposed to possess such power; such power
may have been attributed to him; but I have found no
evidences of it. And, in truth, I have not been able to
discover that it was held that his land was in any way
different from what we find this lower world at this time,
so far as physical phenomena may indicate.

This chief was, in a sense, the progenitor of the people
of our world as known to the ancient Wyandots. But
these people were " created " by his grandsons, the Twins,
the sons of his daughter, the Woman who fell from heaven.
By all that I have heard, he was surpassed in power by
these grandsons, the Twins, and especially in matters
pertaining to this world.

THE GOD OF NATURE.

The Wyandots had a God of the Forest and all Nature.
His name means " The Great One of the Water and the

Land." He was the deification of the mythical Tsĕh'-stäh, the Good One of the Twins born of the Woman who fell from heaven. His name is only a variation of the name of Tsĕh'-stäh, with the attribute of greatness added.

The Wyandot God of Nature was the Jouskeha of the Hurons. The Wyandot and Huron accounts of his birth differ. Parkman identifies him with the Sun. The Wyandots explain the creation of the sun by a different myth. They say the sun was made by the Little Turtle, at the instance of the Animals in Council assembled. But the God of Nature, notwithstanding, was the most important God of the Wyandot Mythology. He made the corn, tobacco, beans and pumpkins grow; he provided fish and game for the people. I find, however, no evidence anywhere that the Wyandots worshipped him at any time, or at any period of their history. His place of abode was not definitely fixed by them, although he was supposed to live somewhere in the East. They thought that he often manifested himself to them, being seen in the forests, fields, lakes and streams. If the stalk of corn seen in his hand was full-eared, well-grown, and perfectly grained, a bountiful harvest was indicated; but if it was blasted and withered, no corn was to be expected, and famine was imminent. If he carried in his hand the bare bone of fish or game, it was certain that none of either could be taken or killed for a season. If, pale and gaunt, he entered any village gnawing the shrunken, withered limb of human being, he thereby foretold famine so dire that many Wyandots must perish from hunger and plague before it was stayed. But I could not learn that it was ever supposed or held that he caused, or that he could prevent, the visitation of the impending catastrophe.

THE WAR GOD.

The ancient Wyandots had a War God. The only translation of this name that I could ever get is,

" Warrior not afraid," or

" Warrior not afraid of Battle."

He was a deity of much consequence to the Wyandots, but I have been unable to learn from them anything whatever in relation to his origin. If he had not been previously offended, victory was sure to rest with the Wyandots, regardless of the stress to which they had been pushed by any of the adverse circumstances of battle; but if offense had been offered him, no victory, but defeat only, could be had until a propitiation had been made. I found nothing to signify that he ever required, as a propitiation, human sacrifice, under even the most extreme provocation, although the Wyandots undoubtedly tortured prisoners of war in ancient times. Writers accord the Wyandots the highest place for bravery in battle. They were also exceptionally humane in their treatment of captives, the leading families in numbers and influence in the tribe since Wayne's victory being those founded by white prisoners that were adopted by them. It is possible that they were influenced in both instances by their faith in their God of War.

There is nothing in the name of this War God to identify him with Areskoui, the War God of the Hurons, although it is very probable that they are identical. It is said that he has been identified with the sun, and he is, perhaps, to be regarded as the God of Nature under different attributes.

THE GOD OF DREAMS.

The Wyandot had a God of Dreams. The name signifies

" The Revealer," or

" He makes the Vision," or

" He makes the Dream."

He was supposed to have something to do with the supernatural influences that acted upon this life, and he revealed the effects of these influences to the Wyandots in dreams. All visions and dreams came from him, for he had control of the souls of the Wyandots while they slept or were unconscious from injury or from disease. The medicine man could detach his soul from his body and send it to the God of Dreams for information at any time, and during its absence he was in a trance-like condition. As all dreams and visions were considered direct revelations from the Dream God, they were regarded as of the very highest significance and of the first importance. No God of the Wyandots was held in higher esteem—no other exerted so great an influence directly upon their social institutions as the God of Dreams. Even to this day the Wyandots attach supreme significance to their dreams.

Under the name of Tarenyowagon or Teharonhiawagon this God was recognized by the Iroquois proper, or Five Nations. I find no account of any god of this name among the Hurons, although from the known importance which they attached to dreams he was probably a Huron God also, but with some different name from that given him by either the Wyandots or the Iroquois.

THE THUNDER GOD.

Hēh'-nŭh was the Thunder God of the Wyandots. By some accounts he came into the world with the Woman who fell from heaven. The thunder is only the voice of this God, and it is called hēh'-nōh. Hēh'-nōh was a God much in esteem with the Wyandots; he was always rendering them some service or showing them some favor—fighting for them—slaying some monster—or sending rain. He liked to dwell about the streams and lakes, and especially about the cataracts or waterfalls which "had a loud voice," i. e., which made a continuous and deafening roar. He lived for ages in the caverns behind Niagara Falls. When he left that place he is supposed to have gone to some unknown point in the far Northwest to seek a permanent home. For this reason the West Wind is defied by the Wyandots; they believed it was sent them by Hēh'-nōh directly from his dwelling-place; and that he rode in the thunder-heads which it wafted along the sky.

The Wyandots relate the same legend of the residence of Hēh'-nōh at Niagara Falls that is told by the Senecas. The variation is very slight, really little more than would be made by different members of the tribe of Senecas.

THE ANIMALS.

The Wyandot mythology endowed the ancient Animals with great power of the supernatural order. This is especially true of those Animals used by them as totems or clan insignia, and from whom they were anciently descended. Of the Animals, the Big Turtle stands in first place. He caused the Great Island (North America) to grow on his back, for a resting-place and home for the Woman who fell down from heaven. He is supposed to carry the Great Island on his back to this day.

The Little Turtle is second in rank and importance in the list of Animals. By order of the Council of these Animals he made the Sun; he made the Moon to be the Sun's wife. He made all the fixed stars; but the stars which "run about the sky" are supposed to be the children of the Sun and Moon. The Sun, Moon and Stars were made for the comfort and convenience of the Woman who fell from heaven. To do this it was necessary for the Little Turtle to go up to the sky, and this difficult matter was accomplished by the aid of the Thunder God. The Deer was the second Animal to get into the sky; this he did by and with the assistance of the Rainbow. And afterward all the other totemic Animals except the Mud Turtle went up to the sky by the same way, and they are supposed to be living there to this present time. The Mud Turtle is appointed to rule over the land of the Little People, in the interior of the earth. The Animals seem to have governed the world before the Woman fell from heaven, and for some time after that important event. Among the Animals mentioned by the Wyandots as living here before the Woman's advent are the Big Turtle, the Little Turtle, the Toad, the two Swans, the Otter, the Beaver, the Snake, the Bear, the Wolf, the Hawk, the Deer, the Porcupine, the Muskrat, and many others. Where and how the land animals lived when all was covered with water is not explained. In the ancient mythology these land animals may have been absent or wanting until after the creation of the Great Island, but I heard them spoken of as contemporaneous with the Turtles, the Toad, and the Swans.

THE WOMAN THAT FELL FROM HEAVEN.

The Woman that fell from heaven is an important personage in the Wyandot mythology. No supernatural powers were attributed to her while on earth by any legend I ever heard from the Wyandots. She has no name, that I have been able to discover.

As to the cause of her falling into this lower world, the Wyandot myth leaves it to be inferred that it was purely an unfortunate and unexpected event of accidental nature —unfortunate for her father, who thereby lost a daughter, but very fortunate for the Wyandots and all after-dwellers in this lower world. The Animals devised the Great Island and the lights in the sky for her convenience and comfort. After the birth of the Twins nothing more is heard directly of her in connection with this world. But that she remained here is to be inferred, for in the great Yōōh'-wäh-täh'-yōh she had charge of the Wyandots while her son went forth to re-create the works of the world. She was directed by her father what to call the Twins, and the myth leaves the inference that she brought them up, but I was never able to get any positive statement to that effect. She is again unlike the Huron Eataentsic in having nothing to do with the destinies of the world and its inhabitants. The Wyandot mythology ignores the mother of the "creator" of the Wyandots, after the birth of the Twins, so far as this life is concerned. This might be explained by contending that the myth as heard at this day is incomplete and fragmentary. This may be, but I think it more probable that after the birth of the Twins, no further consideration in this life was accorded the Woman that fell from heaven. She was assigned a station in the great underground city or Yōōh'-wäh-täh'-yōh, to assist the souls of all dead Wyandots on their way to the land of the Little People.

On the Great Island this Woman that fell down from heaven found living an old woman who took her to live with her in her lodge, and whom she called Shōōh'-täh'-äh, i. e., her Grandmother. Her sole office seems to have been to furnish a home to the Woman that fell from heaven— a lodge, a home.

THE TWINS.

Their names were bestowed by direction of their Grandfather, the Mighty Ruler. One was Good, the other Evil.[1] The Good One was called by the name which means " Man made of fire." The Bad One was called by a name which means " Man made of Flint." These names are too long and unpronounceable to be written in a work of this character. In their stead we shall use the Wyandot words for " fire " and " flint " for these names. This makes the name of the Good One Tsēh'-stäh, and the name of the Bad One Täh'-wĕh-skäh'-rĕh. These words are not the Wyandot names, but are used in this work for them.

The ancient Wyandots ascribed the world as modified for their use, to the supernatural powers and efforts of

---

[1] The terms "good" and "bad" as applied to these brothers do not express moral good and evil as we understand these principles. It might be said that they more properly express the ideas, Friend and Enemy. A moral good and evil might have developed from these ideas. They embraced the fundamental ideas of such, and contained the germs of a moral good and evil.

these Brothers, the Twins. Brinton says, "In effect a myth of creation is nowhere found among primitive nations." The Wyandot mythology does not begin until there is something to begin with, and so far as the creation of the world is concerned no attempt is made to account for it in the condition we first see it when the Swans were swimming about in the Great Water. The Great Island was made by the Big Turtle, of earth that fell down from heaven with the Woman, and the myth says that it was enlarged by the brothers, and that they " created " the people—Indians found upon it. In this matter of the creation of peoples, perhaps the greater number of accounts say that the brothers brought them from the land of their Grandfather. But the Wyandot begins with the fall of the Woman from heaven, the world above ours, down to this. There existed two worlds, then, when he begins,— the one we now inhabit, and heaven. Heaven is, of course, not a Wyandot term. This old Wyandot word means " The world beyond the sky," and has always meant just that, but the Christian has taken it to represent his heaven. In this sense the ancient Wyandot did not use it. To him it did not represent a country in which he was to sojourn after death, in a state of bliss, if he was a good Indian here. In his belief this upper world was then precisely what the Great Island was before the coming of the white man, except that it was peopled with Wyandots only. The lower world was a watery waste, so far as Wyandot knowledge extends. If we can believe Morgan, the same thing can be affirmed of the Senecas. There was no sun, no moon, no stars. But the animals dwelt here. Cusick gives the same account for the Tuscaroras. What was accomplished in the way of world creation was some wonderful things performed with material found already at hand.

As to the final fate of the brothers, accounts differ. In some the Bad One was slain by the Good One during the war between them and the people they had created, under their respective leaderships. Some forms of the story have it that he was banished to some other world. That he was slain in a battle with his brother (and by his brother in single combat) is perhaps the most ancient and correct belief. The Good One is supposed to dwell yet at some unknown place in the far East, on the shores of the Great Water.

The Wyandot account of the enlargement of the Great Island, the creation of men and animals, their destruction and re-creation, is one of the strangest conceptions of the human mind. The myth is orderly in arrangement, clear-cut, strong. It bears the impress of vigorous intellect, and strong national individuality. It is the effort of the untutored savage to account for the world in which he finds himself placed. In the light of modern learning it is absurd and grotesque, but when the circumstances under which it was conceived are considered, it becomes a production of remarkable strength and beauty.

THE LITTLE PEOPLE.

The Little People occupy an important place in Wyandot mythology. Their name signifies " The Twins." This name seems to have been given them for several reasons. First, they were the only people made by Tsĕh-stäh, except the Wyandots, and for this reason the Wyan-

—4

dots called them a Twin People to themselves. Second,
they were created in pairs; and they were born in pairs,
or twins, only. They never operated singly in the accom-
plishment of any enterprise; and only in very rare instances were more than two of them required for the
performance of any task or purpose, however great or
severe. Two of them expelled the Witch Buffaloes from
the Big Bone Licks in Kentucky. The Wyandots claim
that the footsteps of these two of the Little People that
expelled these Witch Buffaloes, and also the impressions
left by them when and where they crouched down, can be
yet plainly seen in the huge masses of stone all over that
part of Kentucky in the vicinity of these Licks. The
Rev. Smith Nichols, a Quaker preacher, a Wyandot, and
Chief of the Deer Clan, also hereditary chief of the
Wyandot tribe, a man of sterling integrity and great worth,
living now in the Seneca country, Indian Territory, in-
forms me that he has not only seen these footsteps and
body-prints, but also the imprints of the little bows and
arrows of the Little People in the solid rock in Ohio, Kentucky, and the Indian Territory. He implicitly believes
that he has.

Tsĕh'-stäh created the Little People to aid him and the
Wyandots to overcome Täh'-wĕh-skäh'-rĕh and his people
in the war in which the first creation was destroyed. They
were of very diminutive size, but they possessed marvelous
supernatural powers. They lived (and they are supposed
to live yet) in stone caves in the bowels of the earth; but
in these caves are forests, streams, game, night and day,
heat and cold, as on the surface of the earth. These Little
People are represented as living precisely as the ancient

Wyandots lived, and as having the laws, customs, social organization, political and religious institutions of the ancient Wyandots, and these it is their task, duty and pleasure to preserve in all their primeval purity for the Wyandots to have and to use in this land, to which they will go after death. The Little People were regarded as the guardians of the Wyandots both in this world and in the world to come. They were supposed by the Wyandots to be constantly fighting the Flying Heads, the monster bears, snakes and other animals of great size that plagued them. They have the power to enter and pass through solid rock, and they always pass through the " living rock " in returning to their subterranean home; and this home is pictured as one of ideal beauty, according to the Indian standard, but no one in all the realms of Indian imagination, natural or supernatural, ever has or ever can see this beautiful country except the Little People, until after death, when it is to be also the abode of the Wyandots. It is ruled now by the Mud Turtle who made it, but at the end of time the Woman who fell from heaven is to take charge of it as ruler.

THE HOOH'-KEH.

The hōōh'-kēh was the " medicine man " of the Wyandots, and the ōōh'-kēh was the " medicine woman." The term " medicine " is, in my opinion, a poor one for the Wyandot expression for which it is used. It seems, however, to be accepted generally, and no better word seems available. The terms hōōh'-kēh and ōōh'-kēh are not, in the Wyandot, restricted to men and women. Anything supposed to possess any supernatural power, or to exert any supernatural influence, was anciently denominated by one of these terms. The office of the " medicine man " was practically the same in the different tribes of the Iroquoian family. Their functions have been so often described that it is unnecessary to repeat them here.

THE MYTHS

I.—SOURCES OF INFORMATION.

The myths are written as I heard them from the old Wyandots. The accounts of some of them differed from the versions of others who repeated these ancient beliefs to me. Some could repeat only the vague and confused outlines of a myth; others could repeat the whole of it, together with many modern additions, modifications and corruptions. I have heard the merest allusion to a myth and then been unable to obtain anything more about it for weeks, sometimes months, and in the case of the Stone Giants it was more than a year from the time I first heard the story outlined until I could get anything like a satisfactory version of it. I sought every opportunity to hear these myths, and became so familiar with them that I could repeat them to the Wyandots better (as they said) than any of them could relate them themselves. I have tried to write out simple statements of the oldest versions that I could hear. After studying well and for years the different versions that I could hear of a myth, and rejecting known interpolations, additions and distortions, and supplying from one account what another lacked, I have told the story as I could see it should be and as I felt that

(53)

it anciently had been. And I have had old Wyandots, after hearing me relate these legends, say with much delight and great satisfaction, " Why, you are more Wyandot than we are." " That story you told like my grandfather told it." " I seemed to hear the words of the old people while you were talking." " My grandmother told that story in the same way when I was a child." Or, " We had forgotten the old stories, and now a white man comes and restores them to us." These and many other expressions of approval I often heard from the old Wyandots in my relation of these myths.

Among the Wyandot people who have been particularly helpful to me in gathering up the fragments of their folk-lore that remain are the following:

GEORGE WRIGHT.

The first place belongs to George Wright. He was a most remarkable man. He had a most remarkable history, too, and at the risk of being tedious I will give here a brief outline of it.

He was a Wyandot only by adoption. His clan was that of the Wolf. His name was Häh-shēh'-träh, and means " The footprint of the Wolf." By blood he was a St. Regis Seneca, his father having been one-half St. Regis Seneca and one-half French. His mother was one-half Delaware and one-half negro.

His grandmother was captured in Guinea, Africa. She and other children were playing about the outskirts of a negro village; suddenly they heard the alarm which denoted the presence of slave-stealers. The children fled, but this little girl was unable to hold way with the larger ones;

she was about six years old, and very small of her age. She was captured by the pursuers, who proved to be a party of French slavers. They carried her to the Martinique Islands, where they kept her for some time; here there were many other negroes, of all ages and both sexes, torn from their homes as she had been. After some time she was taken aboard a ship, which was loaded with her people. The vessel stood out to sea; none of the negroes had any idea of their ultimate destination. When the ship had been at sea a few days it was attacked by the English, and captured. The crew of the French ship were put to the sword; the negroes were carried to America. At Philadelphia Wright's grandmother was sold to a Delaware Indian. She was both slave and wife to the Delaware. Wright's mother was born to her while she was the wife and chattel of this Indian. Sometime during the War of the Revolution this Delaware sold his slave-wife and her daughter to the Rōhn'-tōhn-dēh (or War-pole) of the Wyandots; they were adopted by the Wyandots. Soon after the adoption the daughter was married to the St. Regis Seneca, Wright's father. Wright remembered his grandmother well; he often heard her tell the story of her life.

Wright was born at Upper Sandusky, March 20, 1812. He grew to manhood there and in Canada. He was small of stature, had long straight hair but slightly gray, and a long straight beard a little more gray than his hair. He had a fine face with clean-cut and regular features, with much the appearance of that of a Hindoo sage. He had none of the marks of the negro, but possessed the negro's love of music and delighted to play on his violin, an instrument which he had owned for more than fifty years. He died January 31, 1899, of pneumonia. Until within a month of his death he had always enjoyed the best of health, but had been almost blind for a number of years.

He entered the Indian service under Gen. Lewis Cass, at the age of twenty. His ability made him a valuable man, and he was the best interpreter ever in the service of Gen. Cass, as evidenced by a written statement which the General gave him, and which he treasured for many years. His knowledge of the Indian character made him of great value to the Indian service. His intelligence was of a high order, and he was possessed of some education acquired by his own efforts, and was an extensive reader. He has told me that he was never under the influence of intoxicating liquors in his life.

In 1850 he came to the Wyandots in Kansas. In 1856 his house was accidentally burned, and seeing that the Wyandots would soon have to give up their lands, he went to the Senecas in the Indian Territory, and settled on Sycamore creek, immediately below the Yankee-Bill Prairie, where he lived until his death. This part of the Seneca Reservation was afterwards sold to the Wyandots, who re-adopted him into their tribe, and he was given an allotment of 160 acres, which included his home and improvements. Here he re-entered the Indian service, and was the official interpreter at the Quapaw Agency for sixteen years. He spoke perfect Wyandot, Seneca, Cayuga, Delaware, and Shawnee. His English was good, almost perfect. His discourse was logical, his ideas clear-cut and well defined, orderly, and well arranged.

I often visited him at his home. He was the best in-

formed person in the manners, customs, social organization, political and religious institutions of the ancient
Wyandots, Senecas, Delawares, and Shawnees that I ever
met or became acquainted with. Most of the myths of the
Wyandots which I have preserved I obtained from him,
and the help he gave me enabled me to make some orderly
arrangement of material which I had obtained in so confused form as to be worthless to me. Most that I have
written on these subjects bears the impress of his mind.
Some of the myths are his in entirety. He gave me versions of all of them.

On the day of his death he called to his bedside his
aged wife, and said to her, "I must leave you soon."
Then he carefully smoothed and arranged his long hair
and beard, crossed his hands upon his breast, and died as
peacefully as an infant sleeps.

His sister, Sarah Clark, was born in 1806. She is still
living, and is in good health. I have met her often at his
house. She sews and does other housework without the aid
of glasses. She does not look so much like an Indian as
did Wright, but shows the negro blood plainly.

Wright was well acquainted with Captain Bull-Head,
both in Ohio and Kansas, and gave him credit for being the
best informed man in the old songs, traditions and folk-lore
of the Wyandots that lived in his generation. He often
quoted Bull-Head as infallible authority. Through him I
heard the version of these myths as recited by Captain
Bull-Head. And this brings me to some remarks concerning this most peculiar man.

CAPTAIN BULL-HEAD.

Captain Bull-Head was the purest in blood of any Wyandot that came West from Ohio. He was a genuine Indian in all his ways and inclinations. He died in Wyandotte county, Kansas, about the year 1860. I have made many inquiries concerning his character and mental inclinations, believing that if I could get a full knowledge and a fair comprehension of these I would be in possession of the characteristics of the ancient Wyandot mind as fully as was possible in my day and generation. I have believed that to write intelligently of the ancient beliefs of the Wyandots one should enter into the spirit of the ancient people of that tribe as much as is· possible for one of a different race and environment.

The Captain lived in a house near that of Matthew Brown. This was in a portion of the Wyandot Purchase where those of purest Indian blood settled. The people in this part of the Purchase had little to do with the more progressive portion of the tribe. They gathered themselves together to perform the ancient rites of their fathers. Indian drums, turtle rattles, gourd rattles, the mortar and pestle for grinding corn, the bark boxes for storing hominy for winter use, the tomahawk, the wampum belt, and all other thing valued by the Indian, were to be found here in constant use.

The ancient Wyandot was as sensitive to the various languages of nature as is the highly charged plate of the photographer to the rays of light. The beautiful lines of Bryant apply to the character of the ancient Wyandot:

" To him who in the love of Nature holds
Communion with her visible forms, she speaks
A various language."

Captain Bull-Head was never at a loss for good company. The sky, the clouds, the wind, rain, snow, ice, the
trees, leaves, flowers, the grass under his feet were all
books in which he delighted to read as a child delights in
Jack the Giant-Killer. He carried on communion and
even conversation with the birds, his chickens, pigs, the
wolf, fox, and, indeed, with all Nature, animate or inanimate. And I have often observed this same trait in the
present generation of Wyandots, and, too, in Shawnees,
Delawares, and Cherokees. At the sound of any bird or
animal, Captain Bull-Head made instant reply. These
songs or cries often resemble some sentence of the Wyandot
language. He considered himself addressed, and took up
the conversation at once—much more readily than if he
had been addressed by man.

One day in winter the Captain went out to get some
wood. His chickens were standing close together under
some shrubs, to avoid the wind. When the Captain came
out the rooster flapped his wings and crowed: " Tāh-shāh'-
tāh-dōōhf'-stäh." Now the Captain was dressed in true
Indian style, with blanket and leggings of buckskin. This
sentence supposed by him to have been used by the rooster
means " Your legs are cold." He was highly insulted at
what he imagined the rooster to have said to him, for it
must be remembered the ancient Wyandots endowed all
animals with reason, and he believed the rooster was ridi-
culing him because his thighs were bare.

" Yōōh-äht'!!! " exclaimed the Captain, in a towering

passion. " Yōōh-äht′!!! Sōh-mäh′-äh täh-shäh′-täh-dōōhf′-stäh!″ " "Away! It is your legs that are cold; my legs are not cold; I have been by the fire!″ But the Captain covered his thighs with his blanket and hurried away from the vicinity of the impudent rooster.

At another time the Captain was passing along the road with something in a bag which he had slung across his shoulder. A haughty rooster flew to the top of the fence, flapped his wings and crowed saucily. The Captain believed he said: " Quäh′-zhäh-tschōōh′-těh-quäh.″ This means " You are a peddler,″ or " a man who carries a burden on his back.″ The Captain did not doubt for a moment that the rooster meant to taunt him for turning peddler, than which no higher insult could have been given Captain Bull-Head. He immediately replied, in great heat: " Yōōh-äht′! Sōh-mäh′-äh quäh′-zhäh-tschōōh′-těh-quäh!!″ " No! Away with you! I am not a peddler!″

The little valley in the mouth of which the town of Pomeroy, Wyandotte county, Kansas, stands, was called by the Wyandots, Quěh′-säh-yōhn′-däh, which means " The place where the nettles grow.″ The Captain had friends living there, and his first visit in the spring was to this little valley. One warm day in the spring as he sat in the sun in his cabin door, his favorite rooster came near him and crowed, and the Captain believed he said: " Quěh′-säh-yōhn′-däh.″ In great delight the Captain cried: " Hěhn′-děh′-äh-těhng-däh′-täh-räh quěh′-säh-yōhn′-däh.″ "Ah, yes! You and I will go there to visit soon,″ or "Ah, yes! You and I will soon go there to break bread.″

One class of the songs of the ancient Wyandots consisted

of imaginary conversations with the various animals with which they were familiar. These songs could be sung by two persons, or more. Captain Bull-Head and William Big-Town were famous singers of the old Wyandot songs, and also the old pagan songs in which their history and mythology were wrapped for preservation. With these two men died these ancient songs of the pagan Wyandots. I have gathered the import of some of these mythologic songs as sung by these two men through persons who were intimately acquainted with them—George Wright, Matthias Splitlog and his wife, Eldredge H. Brown, and others. Mr. Brown has given me an account of the manner of their singing, which I shall attempt here to relate.

He heard these songs at the house of Captain Bull-Head, for the Captain possessed the musical instruments necessary for accompaniment. When Big-Town came in sight along the path leading to Bull-Head's home, immediate preparations were made for his reception. A couch was made ready, and when he arrived he was made to lie down, " for," said the Captain, " you must be tired out with so long a walk. Lie here and rest your lungs, your back, your legs. And eat of this meat and drink of this water. Do this and refresh yourself."

While Big-Town rested and refreshed himself, the Captain was engaged in putting his drums and rattles in proper condition for immediate use. When only the two men sang, a little drum the size of a quart measure was used; and the rattle was one made of a small terrapin, or land turtle. If more than the two men were to sing, a larger drum and a larger rattle were used.

When Big-Town had sufficiently rested himself, he was

given the rattle. This instrument he used as a singing-master uses a tuning-fork. He rattled it close to his ear, and when the proper pitch had been ascertained the song was commenced. The songs were almost all arranged for one person or one party to sing, and then to be responded to by the other person or the other party. Big-Town usually commenced the song; when he had sung a part the response was taken up by the Captain. Big-Town accompanied his part with the rattle and the Captain his with the drum. All the mythological tales and legends were thus arranged to be sung, and also all the traditional history of the tribe, as was much of the clan achievement in battle. Mention has been made of songs concerning animals. Eldredge H. Brown can remember that one of their songs commenced " Täh-wēh'-dēh, täh-wēh'-dēh-kěh-hěh'," which is " Hey, the old Otter! His time is past."

They spent hours, sometimes days, even weeks, in singing these ancient songs. As stated in another place, the only traditional stories and myths preserved are the import but not the language of these old songs. What a loss to science was their loss!

MATTHIAS SPLITLOG.

Matthias Splitlog was the famous " millionaire Indian." His father was a Cayuga-Seneca—his mother a Wyandot. He married Eliza Barnett, a very intelligent Wyandot woman of one of the best families in the tribe. She never learned to speak English, and was one of the few Wyandots that I have known that could not speak enough English to carry on conversation in it.

In the year 1882 I was Deputy County Clerk of Wyandotte county, Kansas, and it was my good fortune to be able to do official justice to Mr. Splitlog, and thereby prevent the Missouri Pacific Railway Company from acquiring the land now occupied by that corporation for round-houses and switching purposes, and known as the " Cypress Yards," for about one-tenth of its value. This favor Mr. Splitlog never forgot; he appreciated it as long as he lived. From that day until his death, fourteen years later, he was my true and tried friend. Both he and his wife were well informed in all the myths, legends, and traditions of the Wyandots. They have related these to me by the hour. Mr. Splitlog was also well informed in the Seneca myths and legends, and he was always careful to explain to me the difference between the Wyandot and Seneca versions.

HIRAM M. NORTHRUP.

The late Hiram M. Northrup, the millionaire banker, of Kansas City, Kansas, married a Wyandot woman, Miss Margaret Clarke, the grand-daughter of Chief Adam Brown. Miss Clarke could speak no English until after her marriage. She knew many of the myths and legends of the Wyandots, but it was seldom that she would relate any of them. Mr. Northrup was particularly anxious that they should be preserved, and at his urgent solicitation Mrs. Northrup sometimes went over some of them with me. But it was in a different way that they were helpful to me in this work. They sought out old Wyandots and brought them to their home for the purpose of having them relate to me the myths and traditions. I have every reason to be very grateful to them for their assistance in the collection of these legends.

MRS. LUCY B. ARMSTRONG.

She was the daughter of Rev. Russel Bigelow, one of the pioneers of Methodism in Ohio, and for some time in charge of the Wyandot Mission at Upper Sandusky. She married John MacIntyre Armstrong, a Wyandot of not more than one-quarter blood, a man of intelligence, education, and worth. He was a religious enthusiast, and unpopular in his tribe, but he was conscientious in his acts. He was a local preacher in the Methodist Church for many years. He translated many Methodist hymns from the English into the Wyandot language; and some of the earliest efforts to reduce the Wyandot tongue to a written form were his, though he accomplished nothing in this field that was permanent. His father was a white man who had been captured when very young, by the Wyandots, on the banks of the Allegheny river. He was adopted into the tribe, and grew up an Indian in habit and nature. He married Sarah, the daughter of Isaac Zane, and John MacIntyre was their second son, and could speak no English until he learned it at the Mission.

From her husband and from many other Wyandots Mrs. Armstrong heard the myths and traditions of the Wyandots. She was a widow for forty years and an estimable woman. She lived in Kansas City, Kansas, and I was well acquainted with her for fifteen years. She was of some assistance to me in the study of the myths of the Wyandots. She always wanted to find some analogy to Christianity in the religious legends.

MRS. SARAH DAGNETT.

Mrs. Sarah Dagnett rendered me much assistance in the matter of the Wyandot language in which the myths were told. When I could find no explanation of a Wyandot term anywhere else, I always referred it to her. If there was enough remembrance of the term yet remaining in the tribe to furnish an explanation, she would get it for me. She is a Wyandot and a woman of great intelligence, and has traveled extensively and is well informed.

ELDREDGE H. BROWN.

Mr. Brown is a descendant of Chief Adam Brown, and a man of much worth and integrity. He is the only Wyandot living who understands the old Wyandot language. He has related some myths to me, and has aided me in many ways.

REV. SMITH NICHOLS.

Mr. Nichols is a minister of the denomination of Friends. He is a very conscientious man, and a devout Christian. He has been of much service to me in this work.

HON. SILAS ARMSTRONG.

Mr. Armstrong aided me in many ways in my work. He is a man of fine mind, and great force of character. He has been employed by the Government for several years.

MR. AND MRS. ALFRED MUDEATER.

Mr. and Mrs. Alfred Mudeater are well informed Wyandots, and were always anxious to assist me. I am under obligations to them for many favors.

—5

I have here briefly indicated the principal sources from which I procured the myths and traditions of the Wyandots as they are written herein. I may have misunderstood some things. In the recording I may have perverted and distorted other things. It would be remarkable if I had not erred in some part of the work. Perfection is not claimed. But I have industriously sought to preserve these ancient myths and legends in the interests of science. I may add that no other forms of these legends and myths can ever be obtained, for, with one exception, those pretending to recite *any* form of them are dead, and gone to the Land of the Little People.

THE STORIES

I.—THE WOMAN WHO FELL FROM HEAVEN.

The people lived in heaven. They were Wyandots. The Head Man's name was the Big Chief, or the Mighty Ruler. He had a very beautiful daughter. She became sick. The medicine man came. She could not be cured by his "medicine." He said, "Dig up the wild apple tree; what will cure her she can pluck from among its roots." This apple tree stood near the door of the Lodge of the Mighty Ruler.

The medicine man advised that while they were digging up the wild apple tree they should bring the young woman and lay her down upon the ground under its branches, so that she might see down where the men were at work,[1] and the more quickly pluck away the "medicine" when it should be reached.

When they had dug there for awhile, the tree and the ground all about it suddenly sank down, fell through and disappeared. The lap, or tree-top, caught and carried down the young woman. Tree and woman disappeared, and the rent or broken world, and the rent earth was closed over both of them.

This point where the tree sank down through heaven is

---

[1] Some versions say women were doing the digging; others use the word "people."

called in the Wyandot mythology, the point of breaking through. In some versions of this account it is called the "Jumping-off Place"; for the woman is represented as jumping or springing from the sky. The same Wyandot term is used, though, in all versions.

Underneath, in the lower world, was only water—the Great Water. Two Swans were swimming about there. These Swans saw the young woman falling from heaven. Some accounts say that a mighty peal of thunder, the first ever heard in these lower regions, broke over the waters, and startled all the Swimmers. On looking up, the Swans[1] beheld the woman standing in the rent heavens, clad in flames of bright lightning. She was taller than the highest tree. Thus was she accompanied in her fall from heaven by Hēh'-nōh, the Thunder God of the Wyandots.

One of the Swans said:

"What shall we do with this Woman?"

The other Swan replied:

"We must receive her on our backs."

Then they threw their bodies together, side by side, and she fell upon them.

The swan that had first spoken said:

"What shall we do with this woman? We cannot forever bear her up."

To this question the other Swan replied:

"We must call a Council of all the Swimmers and all the Water Tribes."

This they did. Each Animal came upon special invi-

---

[1] The Wyandot word for swan is used in this place, but the description of the birds would seem to indicate gulls, or geese. They are described as "flat-backed birds," half-a-tree tall; *i. e.*, very large.

tation. The Big Turtle came by special invitation to preside over the Great Council.

Much discussion was had by the Great Council. But it seemed for a long time that the deliberations would be fruitless. No plan for the disposition of the Woman could be agreed upon. When the Great Council was about to adjourn without coming to a conclusion, the Big Turtle said:

"If you can get a little of the Earth, which, with the Woman and the tree, fell down from heaven, I will hold it."

So the Animals took it by turns to try to get the Earth. They dived down into the deep where the tree had fallen. But they could get none of the Earth, which, so the Wyandots claim, shone with a brilliant light to guide them. In this search many of the Animals were drowned, and came to the surface dead. When it seemed that none of the Earth could be obtained, the Toad volunteered to go down and try and see what success she might have.

The Toad was gone a long time. The Great Council despaired of her coming back again. Finally she came up, with her mouth full of the Earth; but she was dead when she reached the surface.

There was very little of the Earth—too little, it was supposed—and the Great Council was discouraged. But the Little Turtle urged that it be used. She rubbed it carefully about the edges of the Big Turtle's shell, and from this small amount soon there was the Great Island upon the Big Turtle's back.

The Woman was removed from the backs of the Swans to the Great Island, which was, from that time, her home.

The Toad was the only Swimmer that could get the

Earth. This is why the Toad has always been called Māh'-shōōh-täh'-äh—Our Grandmother—by the Wyandots. The Toad is held in reverence by the Wyandots, and none of them will harm her, to this day.

II.— THE GREAT ISLAND.

The Island grew to be a Great Land — all of North America, which to the Wyandots was all the land of the earth. The Wyandot name for the Great Island means, literally, "The land which stands up from the Great Water"; but it is correctly rendered "The Great Island." It rests yet on the back of the Big Turtle. He stands deep down in the Great Water, in which the Swans were swimming when they saw the Woman fall from heaven. Sometimes he becomes weary of remaining so long in one position. Then he shifts his weight and moves (changes) his feet. And then the Great Island trembles, and the Wyandots cry out, " He moves the earth! He moves the earth! "

Thus does the Wyandot account for the earthquake.

III.— THE LITTLE TURTLE IN THE SKY, OR THE CREATION OF THE SUN, MOON, AND STARS.

When the Great Island was made on the Big Turtle's back there was no sun, and no moon, and no stars. The Woman could not see well by the " Snow Light." A Great Council was called to see what should be done for a light for the Woman.

After a long time spent in deliberation to no purpose,

the Council was about to disperse and let the world continue in darkness. And now the Little Turtle said:

" Let me go up to the sky; I will put a light there for the Woman."

It was agreed that the Little Turtle might go into the sky. A great Cloud was called by the Council. The Cloud was full of Thunder and Lightning. It rolled over the Great Water. When it came where the Council was in session, it was seen to be full of bushes, trees, streams, lakes and ponds. The Little Turtle got into these streams and was soon carried into the sky, which the Wyandots believed to be solid, and much like the earth at the present time. Here the Little Turtle took some of the Lightning and kindled a great flame, which stood still in the sky. But it did not light all the Great Island, while in that part of it where the Woman lived the heat was intolerable.

The Sun as made by the Little Turtle was not satisfactory. Another Council was called. The Little Turtle came in the Cloud. At this Council it was determined to give the Sun life and a spirit, so that it could " run about the sky." The Mud Turtle was directed to dig a hole clear through the earth (the Great Island), so that the Sun could go through the sky by day, and then, through the hole in the earth, back to the east by night. This the Mud Turtle successfully did. But it seems that the Sun often loitered in this subterranean passage-way, and remained there for long periods. The world was left in total darkness at these times. It was resolved to call a third Great Council to deliberate upon the matter, and to chide the Sun.

To this third Council came the Sun, the Little Turtle, and the other Animals. The Council decreed that the

Little Turtle should make the Sun a wife, and that she should shine while he was going back to the east through the subterranean passage-way made by the Mud Turtle. The Little Turtle made the Moon for a wife for the Sun. Many children were born to them, and these are the Stars that "run about the sky," as the Wyandots call the stars that move like the sun and moon.

After a time the Sun was displeased with his wife, the Moon. He drew her into the subterranean passage-way, and would have destroyed her there if the Little Turtle had not come and rescued her. He robbed her of all her heat and much of her light, and so maimed her that she could not keep pace with him in the sky. The New Moon represents all that was left of the Sun's wife when the Little Turtle rescued her from her husband's wrath. The Little Turtle cured her to that degree that she regained gradually her original form; when, however, she had attained this, she immediately sickened from grief because of her husband's inattention and neglect, and pined away, diminishing daily until she altogether disappeared. When next seen she was again of the same size and form as when rescued by the Little Turtle; then she increased gradually, animated with the hope that when she had reached her former fullness she could recover her husband's favor. Failing in this, she again wasted away; and this has been repeated over and over to this day; and it always will be until the end of time. To assist her in lighting the earth at night the Little Turtle made many lights and fastened them to the sky; these are the fixed stars that have no course, and which do not "run about the sky." Sometimes

they fall off the sky; thus does the Wyandot account for
the meteors or "shooting stars."

From her labors in the heavens and the important functions which the Little Turtle exercised, she was called
Wäh-trŏhn'-yŏh-nŏh'-nĕh, "The Keeper of the Heavens,"
or "She who takes care of the Sky." This is still a name
for women in the Little Turtle Clan of the Wyandots, and
perhaps the oldest name belonging to this Clan. Mrs.
Nancy Stannard, on the Wyandot Reservation, Indian Territory, is of the Little Turtle Clan, and is so named.

The Wyandots believe the comet is the cloud in which
the Little Turtle went up to the sky, burnished and bright-
ened by the Little Turtle with rays taken from the mid-
day sun." In this she rides through the heavens to perform
her duties. About 1882 there was a large comet, visible in
Kansas City, Kansas. It could be seen only in the early
morning. On my way to my office very early one morning,
late in the fall, I met Matthias Splitlog. From where we
stood we had a splendid view of the comet. "See!" said
Mr. Splitlog, "there is the chariot of our Grandmother,
the Little Turtle." Then he told me why it was so called.

IV.— THE TWINS BORN.

The Great Island was the Woman's home. It was not
then so large as it afterwards was made. The Woman
went all about the Great Island. She was very sad. But
in her wanderings she found a Lodge, and, living in it, an
old woman. She called the old woman Shŏŏh"-täh'-äh—
"her Grandmother." In the Wyandot mythology the point
where the Lodge of the old woman stood is called by a Wy-

andot word which means " The place where the Woman
that fell from heaven met (or found) her Grandmother."
The Woman lived with her Grandmother. She is well
now, her sickness having disappeared. To her were born
the Two Children—The Brothers—The Twins. Of these
Children, one was Good—the other Bad. Their Grandfather, the Mighty Ruler, directed how the Twins should
be named. The Good One was named Tsĕh'-stäh—i. e.,
Made of Fire, or the Man who was made of Fire. The Bad
One was named Täh'-wĕh-skäh'-rĕh—i. e., Made of Flint,
or The Man who was made of Flint.

V.— THE GREAT ISLAND ENLARGED.

The Twins grew to manhood after awhile. Täh'-wĕh-
skäh'-rĕh did evil continually. Tsĕh'-stäh was unwilling to
resist his brother continuously, although when he chose to
do so he could overcome him. That all cause for the actions of Täh'-wĕh-skäh'-rĕh might be removed, the brothers
agreed to enlarge the Great Island. They successfully did
this. The land in the East was the land of Tsĕh'-stäh; that
in the West belonged to Täh'-wĕh-skäh'-rĕh. But the land
was desolate—a solitude. Besides the Woman and the Two
children, only the Animals lived upon it.

VI.— THE MODIFICATION OF THE GREAT ISLAND.

When the Twins had finished enlarging the Great Island
they made a further agreement to prepare it for the habita-
tion of man, and other animals than those first found here,

Each brother was to go through his own land.[1] He was to make his realm to conform in surface, animals, birds, streams, lakes, plants, etc., to his own conceptions of utility and beauty. The works of each were to be subject to the modification of the other, but neither was to absolutely change the character of any work of the other, nor was he to totally destroy it.

Each brother now went his way, and did that which was proper in his own eyes. They were engaged in this work for untold ages. When their works were finished, they met again as they had agreed.

When Täh'-wĕh-skäh'-rĕh inspected the works of Tsēh'-stäh he believed they were much too good. Accordingly, he diminished their good qualities to the utmost of his power.

The animals, birds and fishes good for food are the gifts of Tsēh'-stäh. They, and all other animals, were made gentle, harmless. Tooth nor claw was ever made to be turned upon the Wyandot; no animal thirsted for his blood. In lieu of their gentle natures, Täh'-wĕh-skäh'-rĕh made them to have wild and fierce dispositions. He frightened them until they fled from the light of day and only left their lairs at night. The gentle undulations of the park-like woods were changed to rough hills and endless mountain ranges; and rocks, thorns, bushes, briers and brambles were scattered broadcast to plague the Indian. He sprinkled his own blood over the land, and each drop of it made a ragged flint-stone which lay in wait to rend and

---

[1] Whether the modern opinion that the land was divided into Eastern and Western divisions is correct or not, we cannot now tell. The descriptions of the divisions would seem to indicate that they were in fact North and South divisions. I have followed what the Wyandots told me.

cut the Indian's foot. Water would not drown, but Täh'-wĕh-skäh'-rĕh gave it an evil spirit to make it take the life of the Indian. Evil spirits were placed at many water-falls to drag down and destroy Wyandots. The maple tree furnished a pure syrup, but Täh'-wĕh-skäh'-rĕh poured water over the tree and reduced its sweetness to what we find it at this day. Tsĕh'-stäh made the corn plant. It grew without cultivation, and a hundred ears were found upon a single stalk. Täh'-wĕh-skäh'-rĕh made it difficult to raise, and but a few ears were permitted to grow on one stalk. The bean-pod grew upon a tree, and was as long as the Indian's arm; it was filled with beans as large as the turkey's egg, and which were richer than bear's fat. The tree was dwarfed to a helpless vine, and the pod was so re-duced that it was no longer than the Indian's finger. But the wrath of Täh'-wĕh-skäh'-rĕh rose into fury when he be-held the rivers as made by Tsĕh'-stäh. They were made with two currents, flowing in opposite directions, one by each bank, so that the Indian could go either up or down the streams without the labor of paddling his canoe. Täh'-wĕh-skäh'-rĕh thrust his big hand into the river and gave the waters a great swish or splash and mixed them, forcing both currents into only one, and this he made to run al-ways in but one direction.

Tsĕh'-stäh found the works of Täh'-wĕh-skäh'-rĕh much too large and very bad. Bare mountains of rock pierced the sky. Endless swamps and quagmires were spread abroad. Huge beasts, reptiles, birds and insects were at every point to terrify and destroy the Indian. The North Wind stood guardian of the land, and with snows and bit-ter blasts swept this western world. Icicles miles and miles in length hung from the ragged cliffs. Myriads and millions of mosquitoes, each as large as the pheasant, swarmed up from the fetid marshes of the South. Nothing was Good—everything was Bad. All the works of Täh'-wĕh-skäh'-rĕh were modified and their evil qualities reduced to the utmost degree to which he could go by Tsēh'-stäh. But whatever of evil there is in this world comes from Täh'-wĕh-skäh'-rĕh and his wicked works.

The North Wind is still a wicked deity of the Wyandots.

VII.— THE DEER AND THE RAINBOW, OR HOW THE ANIMALS GOT INTO THE SKY.

The Animals were greatly distressed and much offended by the works of Täh'-wĕh-skäh'-rĕh. They saw how fortunate was the Little Turtle, who spent most of her time "Keeping the Heavens." She always came, to attend the Great Council, in the Black Cloud in which were the springs, ponds, streams and lakes.

One day the Deer said to the Rainbow:

"Carry me up to the sky. I must see the Little Turtle."

The Rainbow did not wish to comply with the request of the Deer at that time, but wished to consult the Thunder God about the matter, and so replied:

"Come to me in the winter when I rest on the mountain by the lake. Then I will take you up to the house of the Little Turtle."

The Deer looked and waited all winter for the Rainbow; but the Rainbow did not come. When the Rainbow came, in the summer, the Deer said:

" I waited for you all winter, on the mountain by the lake; you did not come.   Why did you deceive me? "

Then the Rainbow said:

" When you see me in the Fog, over the lake, come to me; then you can go up.   I will carry you up to the house of the Little Turtle in the sky."

One day the Fog rolled in thick banks and heavy masses, over the lake.   The Deer stood on the hill by the lake, waiting and looking for the Rainbow.   When the Rainbow threw the beautiful arch from the lake to the hill, a very white and shining light flashed and shone about the Deer. A straight path, with all the colors of the Rainbow, lay before the Deer; it led through a strange forest.   The Rainbow said:

" Follow the beautiful path through the strange woods."

This the Deer did. · The beautiful way led the Deer to the house of the Little Turtle, in the sky.   And the Deer went about the sky everywhere.

When the Great Council met, the Bear said:

" The Deer is not yet come to the Council; where is the Deer ? "

Then the Hawk flew all about to look for the Deer; but the Hawk could not find the Deer in the air.   Then the Wolf looked in all the woods; but the Deer could not be found in the woods anywhere.

When the Little Turtle came, in the Black Cloud, in which were the streams, the lakes and the ponds, the Bear said:

" The Deer is not yet come to the Council; where is the Deer ?   There can be no council without the Deer."

The Little Turtle replied:

" The Deer is in the sky. The Rainbow made a beautiful pathway of all her colors for the Deer to come up by."

The Council looked up to the sky and saw the Deer running about there. Then the Little Turtle showed to the Council the beautiful pathway made for the Deer by the Rainbow. All the Animals except the Mud Turtle went along the beautiful way, which led them up into the sky. They remain there to this day. They may often be seen, flying or running about the sky.

From this myth, the Deer is sometimes spoken of as Dĕh'-hĕhn-yähn'-tĕh—" The Rainbow," or more properly, " The path of many colors made for the Deer by the Rainbow." This is one of the oldest names for men in the list of names belonging to the Deer Clan. It is one of the names of the writer.

VIII.— PEOPLE BROUGHT TO THE GREAT ISLAND.

When the Animals went into the sky, the world was in despair. The Mountains shrieked and the Earth groaned continually. The Rivers and the Great Water rocked to and fro in their beds, and all the beasts cried aloud for their Mothers, the Animals. The Trees wept tears of blood and the Four Winds rent one another in madness and wrath.

Tsĕh'-stäh and Täh'-wĕh-skäh'-rĕh met to devise a plan to people the Great Island. The place where this meeting was held (it is called a Council, in the Wyandot) is called the Point of Separation; for the Wyandots say it was held on the line separating the land of the Good Brother from the land of the Bad One. The Wyandots came afterwards to believe that the Mississippi river was this line. The descriptions given by the Wyandots would seem to point to Northern and Southern divisions instead of Eastern and Western. I have followed the Wyandots in this matter, although it seems that they were in error as to what the ancient belief actually was upon this subject.

The agreement as finally made between the Twins provided that they should bring people to the Great Island from the land of the Mighty Ruler in heaven. Each was to people his own land, and rule over it without interference from the other.

Tsëh'-stäh brought to his land Wyandots only.

Täh'-wĕh-skäh'-rĕh brought with him many kinds of people, some good and some bad. Some accounts say that the Brothers created these people outright.

The people of each Brother multiplied. In time they became many peoples.

IX.—THE FIRST WAR AND THE FIRST WORKS OF THE GREAT ISLAND DESTROYED.

The ancient compact between the brothers was continually violated by Täh'-wĕh-skäh'-rĕh and his people. The result was a war between the brothers and their respective peoples.

This war lasted many ages. So fierce and devastating was it that all the works made by the brothers, in the beginning was destroyed. The Good Brother was so closely pressed by the Bad Brother that he made the Little People to assist him in his warfare against Täh'-wĕh-skäh'-rĕh and his people. By their aid Tsēh'-stäh overcame his wicked brother and his followers. Tsēh'-stäh pursued Täh'-wĕh-skäh'-rĕh when he fled into his own dominions. The former was armed with the horns of a deer; the latter with the flowering branch which he had torn from the wild apple tree, which fell down from heaven with his Mother. When Täh'-wĕh-skäh'-rĕh entered his own land in his flight from his victorious brother, he was bleeding from many wounds inflicted by the horns of the deer in his brother's hands. Where this blood fell upon the ground it was congealed into flint-stones as sharp as knives, to hinder the pursuit of Tsēh'-stäh. But all his resources availed Täh'-wĕh-skäh'-rĕh nothing. He was beaten down to the earth and slain with the horns by Tsēh'-stäh, his brother.

X.— THE RE-CREATION BY TSEH-STAH OF THE WORKS OF THE GREAT ISLAND.

The war had desolated the Great Island. This destruction was caused by the use of fire by Tsēh'-stäh and of the use of the North Wind by Täh'-wĕh-skäh'-rĕh. No means of subsistence were left. To preserve his people until he could re-create the destroyed works of the Great Island, Tsēh'-stäh built the Yōōh'-wäh-täh'-yōh, or great underground City or subterreanean Dwelling, far to the north of Montreal's present site. Into this he led his people, and then went forth to his work of reconstruction. Here the people were in a torpid state, like turtles and toads and snakes in winter. They were lying about the City in all positions, and they retained only a partial consciousness.

—6

The Woman who fell down from heaven ruled over them with her fiery torch given by Hēh-nōh, the Thunder God.

In making these things anew, Tsēh'-stäh could only re-produce them as they were before their destruction in the war, and as they had been left by the modifications of himself and Täh'-wĕh-skäh'-rĕh. This work required an immense length of time. After ages had elapsed, Tsēh'-stäh came back to the Yōōh'-wäh-täh'-yōh. He said the work was done, and that it was yet too new for use. They could not go out until the Earth was ripened by the Sun.

From the point in the Yōōh'-wäh-täh'-yōh where the Wyandots were a glimmering of light could be seen, and Tsēh'-stäh often went to this small opening to observe the progress of the process of ripening which the world was undergoing. His uniform report when he returned from these inspections was that the world was yet too new for use.

After the Wyandots had waited many ages here, the world was ready for their use again. One day in spring Tsēh'-stäh went forth from the Yōōh'-wäh-täh'-yōh by the small opening. He looked about the whole of the Great Island. He saw it was indeed ready to receive the people for whom it had been created, and for whom all the works of Nature cried out both day and night. He returned to the Yōōh'-wäh-täh'-yōh where sat the Woman who fell down from heaven with her torch of fire given by Hēh'-nōh, the Thunder God. He announced to his Mother that the world cried aloud for her children. She said to him: "My son, lead them forth in the Order of Precedence and Encampment. They shall come to me on their journey to the land of the Little People."

Then Tsēh'-stäh caused the Earth to quake and to rock to its foundation. Hēh'-nōh shook the heavens and rolled over the Great Waters with his Thunder. All the sky flamed with his fiery darts. The great Yōōh'-wäh-täh'-yōh was rent asunder. A nation stood marshaled to go forth. They marched to the waiting world. The hills, the waters, the beasts, the trees, the birds and the fishes cried out with welcome to the nation born of the earth in a day. They found the earth decked with flowers, and songs of joy poured out from the forests filled with happy birds.

They found some of the people of Täh'-wĕh-skäh'-rĕh still living on the Great Island. Their preservation is not accounted for.

Here ends the Song of the Creation, as sung by Captain Bull-Head and William Big-Town.

XI.— THE FLYING HEADS.

It has been said that stories of the Flying Heads seem to be exclusively of Tuscarora origin. The supposition that the myths of these monsters are, or ever were, confined exclusively to the Tuscarora people, is certainly erroneous. The Wyandots had many myths concerning the Flying Heads. Their origin is also accounted for in the Wyandot myths.

The origin of the Flying Heads is ascribed to two very different sources by the Wyandot mythology, as recited at this time. Which is the true and ancient myth I cannot say. The first account says that they were made by Täh'-wĕh-skäh'-rĕh to plague Tsēh'-stäh and his people, the Wyandots. The second account is as follows:

Ages and ages ago the Wyandots were migrating from a distant country. They were moving all their villages. In the course of their migration they came to a large river with exceedingly steep and rocky shores. This river belonged to some Giants, and these opposed the crossing of the Wyandots.

These Giants were all medicine men. They were of immense size, being as tall as the highest tree. They lived in the stone caverns under the bed of the river. They were cruel and wicked cannibals.

The Wyandots made canoes and attempted to cross over. When a canoe loaded with Wyandots pushed out into the stream, the Giants thrust up from the hidden depths of the water their huge hands, dragged down both canoe and passengers. The Wyandots were carried to the stone caverns of the Giants, where they were tortured at the fiery stake, and afterwards devoured.

The Wyandots were terrified. They could neither advance nor retreat. A solemn Council was called to deliberate upon their fearful dilemma. At the Council a powerful " medicine " was made, by the aid of which it was learned that the Giants could be captured and destroyed if a ring of fire could be built about them when they came out of their caves under the river.

Upon the same night of the Council, the Wyandots saw, on a high cliff on the opposite side of the river, the Giants dancing about the fires in which they were torturing some Wyandots captured a few days before.

The Little Turtle said:

"I can make a great fire from the Lightning. It will go all about the Giants. How can our warriors cross over the river?"

The Big Turtle said:

"Let the Little Turtle and his warriors get upon my back. I will carry them on the bottom of the river, under the water, and the Giants will not see us."

It was so done. The warriors of the Little Turtle crept about the camp of the Giants. Then the Little Turtle brought the Thunder and the Lightning. The Lightning leaped into a great wall, all about the Giants, while the Thunder bore them to the earth. The warriors of the Little Turtle rushed upon the Giants and seized them.

The Little Turtle carried the Giants to a high rock that overhung the river. Here the head of each Giant was cut off and thrown down into the raging water. But the surprise of the Wyandots, and their dismay also, was great when at the dawning of the day they saw all these Giant Heads rise from the waters, with streaming hair covered with blood which shone like lightning. They rose from the troubled waters uttering horrible screams, screeches and yells, flew along the river, and disappeared.

The Wyandots destroyed the caves of the Giants. They then crossed over the river and continued their journey. They came to the point where Montreal now stands.

The Flying Heads plagued the Wyandots. They were more dangerous and troublesome during rainy, foggy, or misty weather. They could enter a cloud of fog, or mist, or rime, and in it approach a Wyandot village unseen. They were cruel and wicked hōōh'-kēhs and cannibals.

They caused sickness; they were vampires, and lay in wait for people, whom they caught and devoured. They carried away children; they blighted the tobacco and other crops; they stole and devoured the game after the hunter had killed it.

Fire was the most potent agency with which to resist them. The Lightning sometimes killed one. The Little People often helped the Wyandots drive them away from their villages. I could never learn that it was supposed that the Flying Heads were ever either entirely expelled or that they voluntarily departed from the Wyandot country.

XII.—THE GREAT SERPENTS.

The Wyandot myths are not agreed as to the origin of the Monster Serpents. By some versions they are supposed to be some of the monsters made by Täh'-wĕh-skäh'-rĕh. Other accounts make their origin the same as that of the Flying Heads. They say that the bodies of the hōōh'-kēh Giants left on the high rock over the river after their heads had been cut off and thrown down did not die, but remained alive. After the Wyandots had gone on upon their migration these bodies of the hōōh'-kēh Giants wriggled themselves to the edge of the precipice and cast their bodies down into the water. Here they were soon transformed into the Big Serpents—huge snakes of enormous length. They slowly followed the Wyandots in their migration, and plagued and tormented them for ages. Some of them were never killed. They live in the bottom of the Great Lakes to this day. Sometimes they throw the waters into great commotion, which can only be allayed by throwing some offering into the lake.

The rivers joining the Great Lakes are only the worn ways made by these monsters in crawling from one lake to another.

XIII.—THE ORIGIN OF THE SNAKE CLAN OF THE WYANDOTS.

[The following is very nearly the exact wording of Matthias Splitlog in his relation of this legend. George Wright told this almost the same way.]

We will commence this way. The old Woman and her granddaughter lived in a lodge in the pine woods. From the best hunters and greatest warriors of the tribe the Young Woman had offers of marriage. She was haughty, and would speak to none of her people. These women were of the Deer Clan.

So, it seems she (the Young Woman) was wandering about her lodge in the Wilderness of the Pine Woods. She saw in the distance a fine-looking young man. He approached her with insinuating addresses. She desired him much. He carried her away to his own lodge. They lived there for some time. His mother lived in their lodge.

One day she went into the woods. She left him lying down. She came back to the lodge and looked among the skins where he was lying. There was a great heap of snakes. When she looked again there was one snake—a big snake. She cried aloud and was terrified. His mother said to him: " Why did you do this?"—*i. e.,* turn into a snake.

She turned about and fled for life towards the seacoast. When she reached the coast she found a man in a canoe, who told her to jump on board. When she had done so, he paddled at lightning speed for the other shore. This. act of the Young Woman is called Oōh'-däh-tōhn'-tēh— She has left her village. It is the first name in the list for women belonging to the Snake Clan. Mrs. Sarah Daguet, a Wyandot of the Snake Clan, is so named.

When the man and the Young Woman in the canoe had gone some distance they heard the Snake-Man coming in pursuit, calling to his wife and entreating her to return. He came to the water, and waded in a way in his effort to follow her, always crying out to her to return. This act of the Snake is called Kāh-yōōh'-mĕhn-däh'-täh by the Wyandots, and signifies entreating without avail, or crying to one your voice does not reach, or does not affect. This word is one of the oldest names for men in the list belonging to the Snake Clan. James Splitlog of the Wyandot Reserve is so named. He is one of the very few left of the Snake Clan.

When the Snake-Man went into the water in pursuit, the Black Cloud rolled across the sky, and Hēh'-nōh slew him with a fiery dart.

The man with whom she embarked conveyed her safely to the other shore. Upon her arrival there she saw a man who said, " Follow me." He took her to a medicine man. Her children were called Snakes. And from these is descended the Snake Clan of the Wyandots.

This Snake or Snake-Man, was short and heavy, in shape much like the cow-buffalo. He had horns like the Deer. It was supposed that the Snake was given horns as a concession to the clan of the woman he hoped to retain as his wife.

There are several forms of this legend.

XIV.—THE WITCH BUFFALOES.

In the land of Silence, Tseh'-stäh made the largest and most beautiful Spring in all his dominions. This is now the Big Bone Licks in Boone county, Kentucky. It is " the big Spring which flowed in ancient times," and which may be properly rendered " The Great Ancient Spring." The modern Wyandot name for it is Oh'-tseh-yōōh'-mäh, " The Spring of bitter water."

Tseh'-stäh made this spring at this point because here stood the lodge of Shōōh-täh'-äh, with whom dwelt the Woman that fell down from heaven. The Two Children were born here. From this Spring, which was then small, drank " The Man of Fire " and " The Man of Flint," in the days of their childhood.

As enlarged by Tseh'stäh the Ancient Spring was so broad that the eye could not see from one bank to the other. Its waters were so clear that the smallest pebble could be seen at the bottom of its inconceivable depths. Then it was the " Great Ancient Spring." As modified by Täh'-weh-skäh'-reh it was reduced to its present size and became Oh'-tseh-yōōh'-mäh, " The Spring of bitter water."

The Wyandots described these Springs as " the great and ancient Spring where the bones are and where the animals come to drink and to see each other."

Täh'-weh-skäh'-reh made a great drum or gong, of stone

or flint, and put it at these Springs. He put in charge of the Springs the Witch Buffaloes, who made unjust rules and oppressive regulations for the government of the Indians and animals coming to use the waters. Elks were admitted to the Springs; when they had been there a stated time they were forced out, and buffaloes admitted, and so of all the animals. The Witch Buffaloes indicated their wishes, and gave forth their orders and commands by beating on the great drum of flint, which could be heard as far as the Great Lakes.

The Witch Buffaloes are represented as having been as tall as a tree, with horns as long as a man is high. Their horns stood straight out from their foreheads. They are always spoken of in the feminine gender.

So oppressive became the Witch Buffaloes that no animal was free to approach the Springs, and thus were the Wyandots prohibited from lying in wait to slay them for food as they came to drink. Neither were the Wyandots allowed to go there to make salt. Finally the Little People took pity on the Wyandots and resolved to destroy the Witch Buffaloes.

Two of the Little People were directed to go to the Springs to perform this difficult task. It required long preliminary work to make ready for the slaughter. When all was ready they attacked the Witch Buffaloes and slew all but a single one, which they wounded, and which only escaped by so enormous a leap that it passed beyond the Great Lakes at the single bound. After the Witch Buffaloes were killed and expelled, the Little People assembled all the animals and said to them and to the Wyandots, " Drink as you will. We are forever the keepers of the

Oh'-tsēh-yōōh'-mäh." The great number of huge bones found by white men at the Big Bone Licks were the bones of the Witch Buffaloes.

The footprints of the two Little People can be yet seen in the stones all over that part of Kentucky about these Springs. They made them while driving all the Witch Buffaloes to the Springs for slaughter. At some points may be seen also the impressions of their bodies and of their bows and quivers on the stone where they sat or lay down. So say the legends of the Wyandots.

XV.—THE STONE GIANTS.

Like the Flying Heads, the Stone Giants, or Hōōh'-strāh-dōōh', are attributed to two sources. By one account they were descended from the Hōōh'-kēh Giants and the Wyandot women they carried away with them when they fled through the Wyandot camp. I believe it improbable that the Wyandots would ascribe the descent of so obnoxious a people to women of their own blood, and consequently, I believe this conception of their origin must have originated with an alien and unfriendly people. But of this I cannot be sure, for I heard this account from Wyandots only, and more frequently than the other account.

The second account says the Hōōh'-strāh-dōōh' were made by Täh'-wĕh-skäh'-rĕh to assist him in the war he so wantonly and unjustly waged against his brother, Tsēh'-stäh, and wherein he lost his life.

The Hōōh'-strāh-dōōh' were medicine men as well as Giants. They were clad in coats of pliable stone. These garments are represented as covering the body completely. Their stone coats were made by smearing the crude turpentine from the pine tree over their bodies, and then rolling in the dry sand of the shores of the Great Water. This process was repeated until the coats were of the required thickness.

The Hōōh'-strāh-dōōh' were cannibals. They slew the Wyandots for the express purpose of devouring their bodies. They are represented as having been half-a-tree tall, and large in proportion. A Hōōh'-strŭh-dōōh' could eat three Wyandots at a single meal.

There is no account of any particular war between the Wyandots and the Hōōh'-strāh-dōōh'. The Wyandots seem to have been annoyed and plagued by them from time immemorial; and always to have been in terror of them. Sometimes they combined in great numbers and attacked one of the Hōōh'-strāh-dōōh'. If by any great good-fortune a chance arrow reached one of the vulnerable points (eyes, mouth, etc.) the Wyandots were victorious; if no such good-fortune attended them in the unequal combat, a bundle of blood-stained, dripping Wyandot slain was carried from the fatal field on the back of the victorious and bloodthirsty Stone Giant for his supper.

The Wyandots sought the aid of the Little People in an effort to expel or conquer the Stone Giants. After a long contest they were divested of their stone coats, and so far reduced that they did not dare to openly attack the Wyandots again. But they lived in solitary places, and attacked hunters and travelers that slept at night in the woods. A favorite stratagem of theirs was to enter the dead body of some Wyandot that had died, in a solitary

hut, alone. When his friends discovered him, or a belated
traveler stopped at the hut, and slept, the Stone Giant animated the corpse, which stealthily slew and devoured the
unfortunate sleepers. A "medicine" made of the bark of
the dĕh'-täh-tsĕh'-äh, or red-bud tree, was supposed to afford
the Wyandots complete protection from such attacks of
the conquered Stone Giants.

The dĕh'-täh-tsĕh'-äh, or red-bud, was, in a sense, a
sacred tree with the Wyandot people. Its name means
"the fire tree," and when its scarlet bloom flames along the
bleak hillsides in the early spring the Wyandots say that
Tsĕh'-stäh is returning again, and bringing with him the
spring.

XVI.—ORIGIN OF THE HAWK CLAN OF THE WYANDOTS.

The Big Bird was the Ruler or Mighty Chief of all the
Eagles, Hawks, Owls, and other birds of prey, as his name
indicates. He lived on the top of a rock so high that the
clouds shut out all view of the lower world.

A Wyandot Girl was too proud to live with her clan,
the name of which is not now remembered. She was an
orphan, and lived with her grandmother. They lived in
the woods, close to a large open space, or prairie. They
were almost starved, for there was no hunter, and no meat
in the lodge. The Girl was disconsolate and melancholy.
She wandered about the prairie and in the woods.

One day she was walking in the prairie close to the
borders of the forest. Suddenly, as she went along, a
great cloud overshadowed her. When she looked up, be-

hold! the cloud was descending upon her, and with huge claws to catch her! Then she saw that it was the Great Bird Chief.

The Girl ran as fast as she could to the woods near by. There she found a great log which was hollow; she crept into it. The Bird Chief followed her and alighted upon the log. He gave a mighty flap with his immense wings, and the blast caused thereby was a storm that leveled the forest. At the same time he exclaimed "kooh-koohks!" (I will claw!) and his voice was like a thunder-crash. Then he seized the log in his terrible talons, and carried both log and Girl to the top of the precipice where he had his home. He lay the log down upon the edge of the height and shook it to make the Girl come out. But she would not do so.

The Girl waited until the Bird Chief went away; then she came out of the log. She looked about and could see only the clouds beating upon the crag. She could not climb down. She found a large nest upon the crag-top, and in it two young birds, each larger than an elk. All about lay dead deer, buffaloes, and other animals, which the Bird Chief had brought up for his young to eat. She found that the wife of the Bird Chief had been slain and thrown down from the pinnacle-top by him while he was in a fury; and he was compelled himself to catch all the animals used for food by his young.

The Bird Chief was a medicine man, and could assume any form he chose. He came back to his lodge on the top of the rock, in the form of a young man. She was his wife (partner—more properly, friend) there in the clouds, on the pinnacle-top. But she despised him, and longed to escape; of this, however, she had little hope. It finally occurred to her, though, that she might escape by the aid of the young birds. She chose the larger one to aid her. She fed him well, and he grew rapidly. It was not long until he could fly off a way and then return to the rock. She thought her time of escape was approaching.

She watched the Bird Chief narrowly, and had learned by this time when he went away, how long he remained absent, and when he returned. She prepared a short stick. One day when the young bird approached the edge of the rock, she, at the opportune moment, sprang upon his back, and clasped him tightly about the neck. The sudden action of the Girl carried the young bird over the precipice, and away they went, Girl and bird, tumbling down the crag. In a little while the young bird spread his wings, caught himself, and flew. When he did not go down fast enough she tapped him on the top of the head with the stick to make him descend the more rapidly. After awhile she could see the land.

When they were about to get to the ground she heard the Bird Chief coming down in pursuit. The whistling and trumpeting he made in his rage were terrible to listen to. She tapped the young bird's head again and again, and finally got to land. She jumped from the young bird's back, plucked the long feathers from his wings so he could not fly after her, then ran into the thick brush and hid in a hole in the rock.

When the Bird Chief came down to the ground he searched everywhere for the Girl, but could not find her. The young bird was very uncomfortable in these lower regions, and was continually crying out that he wanted to

be carried back to the pinnacle. After a long and fruitless search for the Girl, the Bird Chief heeded the cries
of his helpless son, and, taking him in his talons, circled
about, and finally disappeared in the clouds. Then the
Girl gathered up the feathers which she had plucked from
the wings of the young bird, and carried them to the hut
where her grandmother lived.

The children of the Girl were called Hawks. Each one
was given a feather of those plucked by the mother from
the young bird's wings. These Hawks became the an-
cestors of the Hawk Clan of the Wyandots.

XVII.—HOW THE WYANDOTS OBTAINED THE TOBACCO PLANT.

The village stood by the lake. Clear streams flowed into
the lake from the hills. On the hills were large trees.
The Hawk Clan lived in this village. In the village lived
an old man of the Bear Clan. He had a young wife of
the Hawk Clan. Two daughters were born to them.
When she was twelve years old the first daughter died.
Much grief did her death bring to the Old Man and his
young wife. When the second daughter reached the age
of twelve, she, too, was seized with a fatal sickness, and
soon died, also. And the mother soon died of grief. The
Old Man was left alone in the lodge, in deep sorrow.
But he went about to do good. He was held in much
esteem by all the village of the Hawk people.

One day when the Old Man, and others of the village,
were standing by the lake, a large flock of immense
Hawks, half-a-tree tall, came flying over the blue hills, to

the lake. They wheeled and circled about the lake and its shores. One of their number fell to the ground. It lay on the lake-shore, with its wings thrown above its back like a dove. shot with an arrow. The other Hawks flew about for a short time. They screamed and called to each other. Then they flew back over the blue hills from whence they came.

The visit of the Great Hawks to the lake terrified the people in the village. And those standing on the bank of the lake by the Old Man ran about and called aloud, from fright. The Old Man was not frightened by the Great Hawks. He said, "I will go and see the stricken Hawk that fell down." The people said, "Do not go to the Hawk." But the Old Man replied, "I am old. My life is almost done. The heavens are black. I am full of sorrow. I am alone. It can matter little if I die. And I am not afraid of death. I will see the stricken Hawk."

He went on. The way grew dark. But the Hawk lying on the ground remained before him. As he advanced a great flame swept down and consumed the Hawk. When he came to where it had lain, ashes were all about. Lying in these was a living coal of fire in which he saw his first-born daughter. He stooped to look. He saw it was indeed his daughter. He took her up. She spoke to him. Then the other people of the village came also. The child spoke to them. She said, "I have returned with a precious gift for the Wyandots. I am sent with it to my own clan, the Hawk people."

Then she opened her hands. They were full of very small seeds. These she planted in the ashes of the fire

—7

from which she had risen. Soon a large field of Tobacco
grew from the little seeds.

The Girl lived with her people. She taught them how to
cultivate and cure the Tobacco. She taught them to make
offerings of it, and to smoke it in pipes.

And the Wyandots were thus more fortunate than any
other people. They alone had Tobacco.

[There are other forms of this myth.]

XVIII.—THE LAZY HUNTER WHO WISHED TO GET MARRIED.

Once there was a very lazy and worthless man in a
Wyandot village. He had never killed any game. He
was regarded with scorn by the women, and with indiffer-
ence by the men. When he sought a wife he was answered by the damsel, "No meat can be found in your
lodge; woman likes meat."

The great desire he had for a wife forced him to try
to get some meat for his lodge. On a warm day in summer
he went into the woods about the village with his war-club.
The first animal which he saw was an opossum. This he
slew with his war-club. He seized it by the tail and flung
it over his shoulder; and he marched to the village with
his game. Flies swarmed upon his opossum. In the
village when he stepped over a log or jumped across a
brook the flies rose in clouds and hummed about his ears.
But he believed that the noise of the wings of the flies
was the clamor of the maidens of the village in determining whom of them should have him for a husband, and
in admiration of his prowess as a hunter. However, none

of them accosted him with a proposal to be his wife. At
the extreme edge of the village he met some hunters coming
in with game. To these he complained of his ill success
in getting a wife. The hunters were greatly amused,
and set upon him in so boisterous a way that he threw
down his opossum and fled into the woods. And he is
running about there to this day, in a vain search for
game with which to get a wife.

XIX.—THE TATTLER.

There is a small bird in the Wyandot country, about
the size of and much like the tomtit. He has a light or
grayish head, and black circles around his eyes. The
Wyandots believe him to be a great tattler or tale-bearer—
a mischief-making liar—and that these black rings about
his eyes are the result of injury received from some bird
whom he has harmed by his lying. For this reason the
bird is called Täh′-tēh-zhāh′-ēh-zhäh′-ēh—The Tattler.
A lying man or woman is given this same name by the
Wyandots.

XX.—SUPERSTITIONS.

Many superstitions are believed in to this day by the
Wyandots. Perhaps some of them are those of white
people. Others are of Indian origin.

One of these is the seeing of the soul of a person.
Often persons that are known to be miles away, or to be
sick in bed, are met on the highway, usually at the
crossings of streams; or they are seen walking about the
fields and paths. If they are seen in the forenoon the

omen is good for the person so seen, and the earlier seen the better the omen. But if seen in the afternoon the omen for the person so seen is bad, and if after sunset and before midnight it indicates that the person so seen will die in a short time.

The medicine men and medicine women were supposed to possess the power to assume the form and nature of any animal they chose for the purpose. Under this guise they were supposed to go about the neighborhood and commit such depredations as the animal was capable of. If the animal was killed, the person was killed; if only wounded, the person carried a similar wound. This belief gave rise to the story of

THE BIG DOG.—Once, in Wyandotte county, Kansas, the Wyandots were troubled by the prowling of a vicious dog of enormous size and strength. This dog was seen only at night. Calves, lambs and pigs were killed by it. Any article of household furnishing left outdoors overnight was usually torn and soiled, if not totally destroyed. Belated travelers were attacked and often severely injured. The favorite dogs of the Wyandots were maimed, crippled, killed. Gardens and flower-beds were trampled down and ruined. Smoke-houses were invaded, and hams, shoulders, jowls and middlings carried away. Hencoops were overturned, and havoc played with their feathered occupants. Flocks of geese and ducks were chased, worried, destroyed.

Terror reigned. Lovers did not stroll in the moonlight. Husbands ascertained that they could transact their business in " Kansas," take aboard a reasonable amount of " fire-water," and still reach home before dark. Livestock was housed, and it was observed that "breachy" kine which had before delighted in the nocturnal destruction of a neighbor's crop, huddled close to the yard fences at sunset, and there demurely chewed the cud of content till the sun was well up on the following morning.

Things came to such a pass that Captain Bull-Head was importuned to deliver the people from the pest and nuisance. He made "medicine," and ascertained that this dog was in fact an old woman of the Wyandots, noted for her malevolence and cynicism. He loaded the old British blunderbuss which he had carried in the ranks of Proctor's army in the war of 1812. He loaded it according to the formula prescribed by Wyandot superstition for "witch-killing," for no ordinary bullet and gunpowder had any effect upon witches. The night which followed his preparations was damp and rainy. Sheets of red lightning flared up from the horizon, and a sullen thunder growled and rolled and bellowed in the distance. It was such a night as witches delight to be abroad in. About ten o'clock a hubbub was raised in Captain Bull-Head's pig-pen. He advanced to the rescue, and upon his arrival there the Big Dog bounded out of the inclosure. As it went over the fence the Captain fired, and a terrific howl went up, but the Big Dog disappeared and was never seen again. And lo! the next morning this same old Wyandot woman was found to have a badly wounded foot! And what though she told of falling? The whole community was sure that Captain Bull-Head had shot her as she jumped over the walls of his pig-sty!

XXI.—WHY THE AUTUMNAL FORESTS ARE MANY-COLORED.

The Animals were angry with the Deer for deserting them and forsaking the Great Council to go into the sky. They believed that all should have gone up together.

The Bear was the second animal to go into the sky by way of the beautiful pathway of burning colors laid down by the Rainbow. When the Bear had come up, he said to the Deer:

"Why did you leave us to come into the sky, the land of the Little Turtle? Why did you desert the Great Council? Why did you not wait until all could come with you?"

The Deer said:

"None but the Wolf may question why I came. I will slay you for your impertinence."

Then the Deer arched his neck; he poised his antlered head; the hair stood erect along his back; his eyes blazed with the fires of a fury which burned within him.

The Bear was not afraid. He stood up. His claws were very strong. His hoarse growls sounded along the sky.

The battle of the Deer and the Bear shook the heavens. The Animals looked up from the Great Island. They directed the Wolf to go up to the sky and stop the conflict.

The Wolf made the Deer desist. But the blood of the Bear dripped from the antlers of the Deer as he ran away. It fell down upon the leaves of the trees on the Great Island. Every year when autumn paints the foliage

of the land such beautiful colors the Wyandots say it is but
the blood of the Bear again thrown down from heaven.

[The beauties of the autumn foliage are also accounted for in
another and different story, in which it is said that the Trees wept
tears of blood at the loss of the Animals when they went into the
sky to live permanently. This was in the autumn. At that season of the year the Trees take on these beautiful colors in memory
of that season of deep grief when they wept in an agony of bloody
tears.]

XXII.—ORIGIN OF THE MEDICINE FORMULAS OF THE WYANDOTS.

Like all other Indians, the Wyandots depended for the
cure of diseases much more upon that "medicine" which
consisted in supernatural agencies, than upon remedies
compounded from rational ingredients. The tribe was,
however, in possession of formulas for the cure of some
diseases, wounds, and injuries. Some of these, combined
with the mode of life, vigor of constitution, and scant diet
of the Indian, were of considerable efficacy. They were,
too, of undoubted antiquity. To enhance the potency and
virtue of these formulas, their origin was attributed to a
supernatural manifestation in favor of the Wyandots.
The myth made to preserve this divine interposition and
to perpetuate it in the Wyandot tribe is as follows:

Far to the north of Quebec there is a great mountain.
It is covered with mighty forests, the leaves of which are
always as red as blood. This is the result of the great
quantity of the blood of the Bear which was here thrown
down from the sky in the battle between that Animal and
the Deer. No amount of rain which has fallen in that land

has ever been sufficient to wash away these blood-stains from this mountain, which is supposed to be, in a way, and to some degree, sacred to the bears of this lower world.

A Wyandot and his wife were once going from one village of the tribe to another. When they had ascended the high mountain below which was the lake, they were passing through a deep forest of dark pines. Here they were suddenly surrounded by a great company of Bears, who came tumbling down into the path or trail from the hillside above. There was no opportunity of escape, and as the Bears did not offer to molest them, the man and his wife came to some reassurance. Not only did the company of Bears show no inclination to injure the Wyandots, but to their extreme astonishment the largest Bear, who seemed to be the leader of the company, stood erect on his hinder legs, and said to them:

" You must go with us to our home in the Red Mountains. There you must both remain until it is our pleasure to dismiss you."

The man and his wife supposed that they had fallen into the hands of some very cunning and dangerous hōōh'-kēhs who had assumed the form of the bear. They were much frightened. But as resistance would have caused them to be instantly torn in pieces, they went quietly enough in company with the Bears. These proved no bad companions of the road, either. I suppose no more jolly company of Bears ever lived anywhere, either in the Red Range or out of it. They frolicked by the way, and were continually playing pranks upon each other. They danced in the openings. They tumbled in the dry leaves. They cuffed each other. They turned summersaults on the stretches of soft moss. They rolled down the steep hillsides which came in their way. They made the forests ring with their shouts, their hoarse growls, and their laughter. Indeed, so much like a company of young Wyandots about the village did these Bears demean themselves that the man lost his fear, threw aside his restraint, and joined them in their sports. He received many a rough tumble in the wrestling, many a sound cuff in the boxing, many a mishap in the tumbling. But he took these with such grace and good-humor that it was soon clear that he had gained a high place in the estimation of his captors.

As night was coming on, the Red Range came in sight. Then the Bears set up a great cry of satisfaction. When they came into the midst of the Red Hills they said to the man and his wife:

" You are now in the Red Mountains. These are sacred to the Bears. They are dyed with the blood of our grandfather. A fine cave with plenty of dry leaves in it will be given you for a home. The finest nuts in the world grow here on every side; take them for food. Be content here, for it is impossible for you to go away."

A fine cleft in the rocks was then shown them; they were compelled to live in it. They gathered nuts for food. But they desired to return to their own home in the village of the Wyandots. One day the man said they must try to escape. They fled along the Red Hills. They were pursued and quickly overtaken by a troop of the Bears. " See," said they, " he runs away from those who give him a house and food. He deserves death." And, seizing him, they threw him down from a great height. He was sorely bruised, and all his bones were broken. They took him up and carried him back to the cave given him for a home.

Upon their arrival at the cave the Bears said to the wife that she must gather certain leaves, roots, and barks, which they named to her. This she did, and the Bears told her in what manner to compound them. The sick man was given some of this " medicine," and immediately he was restored to his former good health.

The next day he again attempted to escape from the Red Range. The pursuing Bears came up with him in his flight. They said: " See, he again tries to run away from those who give him a home and meat. He deserves no less than death by our claws." And with that they fell upon him and nearly rent him in pieces with their claws. They bore him to the cave given him for a home. Here the wife was once more directed to gather leaves, roots, and the barks of trees. She was shown how to make " medicine " of them. This she applied to her husband's wounds as directed by the Bears. And he was at once made whole again.

In this manner he was afflicted with many kinds of diseases and injury, and in like manner restored to health. One day the Bears said to him:

" We are friends to our brethren the Wyandots. We desire to show them the way to cure themselves when sick. We have afflicted you and taught your wife how to cure you. She knows how to make all the ' medicine.' Carry this knowledge back to your people. Tell them to honor the bones of the bears slain for food, and without fail to keep in use all the names in the list belonging to the Bear

Clan. Do not suffer any of them to be 'thrown away' or to die from disuse."

After this speech the company of Bears came about them, and they were conducted out of the beautiful Red Range in the same manner in which they were conducted into it. They came to the village of the Wyandots, and made known to them what had befallen them in the Red Mountain Range, and delivered the message sent by the good Bears that dwelt therein. And the formulas brought back by the woman never failed to cure the Wyandots of their ills.

XXIII.—WHY THE DEER DROPS HIS HORNS EVERY YEAR.

In the war between the Twins of the Woman who fell down from heaven Täh'-wĕh-skäh'-rĕh invaded the land of his brother Tsēh'-stäh, who defeated him in a great battle. Täh'-wĕh-skäh'-rĕh said to one of his warriors:

"Bring me the swiftest animal in the forests of Tsēh'-stäh."

It was winter. The warrior brought him the Deer. The Deer was proud of his antlers. He held his head aloft. Täh'-wĕh-skäh'-rĕh said to him:

"This day must I flee from the land of my brother; bear me away on your back."

All the Animals despised Täh'-wĕh-skäh'-rĕh, but they loved Tsēh'-stäh. The Deer said:

"See my great horns; they will hang in the branches of the trees as I run. The Hawk can carry you more swiftly than I."

Then did the rage of Täh'-wĕh-skäh'-rĕh rise.   In his anger he answered the Deer:

"The Hawk would say, 'You are too heavy for my wings'; I will not call the Hawk."

Saying this, he snatched off the Deer's horns, and then said to him:

" Now flee with me to my own land, for my brother is near; he seeks my life.   In my own land I will return to you your horns."

He compelled the Deer to do his will.   But on the borders of his own land his brother was in such close pursuit that Täh'-wĕh-skäh'-rĕh failed to return the Deer his horns; he fled with them in his hands, but dropped them when he escaped.   Tsĕh'stäh picked up the horns to return them to the Deer; but the Deer was humiliated. He did not come forth from the woods until late the next summer, after he had grown another pair of horns.

To this day, when that season arrives in which Täh'-wĕh-skäh'-rĕh broke away the horns of the Deer, the horns of every deer in the forests fall off.   They are replaced by a pair of new ones as soon as they can grow, which is before the end of summer.

Tsĕh'-stäh retained the horns of the Deer for his weapon in war.   In the last battle he slew his wicked brother, Täh'-wĕh-skäh'-rĕh, with these same horns by him so cruelly torn from the head of the Deer.

XXIV.— THE SINGING MAIDENS, OR THE ORIGIN OF THE PLEIADES.

The pleiades have ever been favorite stars with mankind. And they were so with the Wyandots. They believed the constellation consists of six stars, only. The Wyandots account for the origin of this beautiful star-group in the following myth:

The Sun and his wife, the Moon, had many children. Among these were six little girls, the daughters of a single birth. They were beautiful, kind, gentle and loving children. They were great favorites in all the heavens, for they loved to go about and do good. In addition to their other accomplishments, they were the sweetest singers and the most tireless and graceful dancers in all the sky-land. They were called the Singing Maidens.

These sweet singers often looked down to this world. They had compassion on the Wyandots when game was scarce, when the corn was blasted, when famine threatened. One day they said to their father, the Sun:

" Let us go down to visit the Wyandots on the Great Island. We wish to sing and dance in that land."

The Sun said in reply, to his daughters, the Singing Maidens:

" I forbid your going down to the Great Island to sing for man. Remain in your own house. Be content with the heavens."

But when the Sun was gone to give light and heat to the Great Island, these Children of Light, the Singing Maidens, went abroad. They looked down on the Great Island.

They saw the Wyandot villages almost concealed by the beautiful woods on the banks of the lake. The glittering waves rolled in upon the pebble-strewn beach. The blue waters reflected the autumn-colored woods. The gulls, geese and swans floated at rest on the bosom of the lake, or soared lazily aloft. The great crane waded and fished among the water-lilies. Little children ran from the village down to the beaten shores. They were merry on the yellow sands. They swam and splashed in the brilliant waters. Mermaids were not more lovely than these simple children of the forest playing upon the shores of the lovely lake on the Great Island. This enchanting scene moved the Singing Maidens to ecstacy. They cried out:

" Here is a more beautiful land than can be found in the sky. Why should we be restrained from visiting it? Let us now go down and dance with those happy children, and sing among the beautiful trees on the shore of the bright lake."

Then the Singing Maidens came down to the shining sands on the lake-shore. They sang for the happy children, and danced upon the rippling waters. The children were charmed with the Maidens; they clapped their hands; they sang for joy; they ran and danced along the wooded banks.

The music of the Maidens and the sounds of the merry-making children floated through the great trees to the Wyandot villages. The people stood entranced. They said to each other: " What music is this? We have not heard before so lovely a song. . Let us see who visits our children." And they went towards the lake-shore.

When they saw the Singing Maidens, the Black Cloud

of the Little Turtle overshadowed the land. The voice of Hēh'-nōh, the Grandfather of the Wyandots, rolled over the lake in thunder-tones. It was the Keeper of the Heavens come to carry up the truant Singing Maidens.

The Sun was very angry with his daughters for their disobedience. He said to them:

" I will give you a place so far away that you can never again visit the Great Island."

Then he placed them in a distant circuit so far away in the land of the sky that their bright and shining faces can scarcely be seen. They look with love down to the land of man where once they sang on the billowy lake and danced with happy children on the shining shore.

And the Indian mother says yet to her child in the calm and silent twilight: " Be quiet and sit here at my feet; soon we shall hear the Singing Maidens as they dance among the leaves of the trees."

XXV.— THE INDIAN GAMBLERS — AN O'ER TRUE TALE.[1]

" I will stand the hazard of the die."—*Richard III.*

In the summer of 1773, a numerous body of Indians from the Northwest was assembled at Detroit. This place, besides being a military post, well supplied with military stores, was the great mart for the fur trade. The most numerous of these visiting tribes were the Chippewas, the

---

[1] This is a tradition among the Wyandots. It was written out and published in the *Gazette*, of Kansas City, Kansas, by Governor William Walker, long ago, sometime in the sixties or early in the seventies. This is taken from the *Gazette*. It is told in different forms by the Wyandots. The old files of the *Gazette* are mines of information about Kansas affairs and early Kansas history. Hon. Geo. W. Martin is now editor.

Wyandots, and some Pottawatomies and Ottawas resid-
ing on both sides of the river now dividing Michigan from
Canada West.

These annual visits to the British headquarters were for
trading purposes; exchanging their year's hunt for such
necessaries of Indian use as could be supplied by the traders, such as blankets, cloth, calico, tobacco, guns, ammuni-
tion, etc. Many were there for no other purpose than
spending the summer, as our fashionables do at watering-
places, in idleness, and enjoying " fun and frolic." Ball-
plays, foot-races, wrestling, and at night dog feasts (a religious festival among the Chippewas), and dances of
every kind known among them.

The chiefs and head men in the meantime held councils, and smoked the calumet of peace with the English
commandant, to hear the talk of their great father the
King of England, and to receive presents. The women
were employed in tanning and dressing elk- and deer-skins,
cooking, etc.

Games of chance are not, as a passion, confined to civilization, but are indulged in by the wild an uncivilized as
well. Among their rude games is one known as " mocca-
sin." Two only can play at the game. They are seated
face to face on a buffalo- or deer-skin. Four new moccasins
and a rifle-ball make up the implements employed in the
game.

The moccasins are placed nearly equidistant, like a four-
spot on a playing-card. The players, seated cross-legged,
facing each other, now toss up for the ball or first " hide."
The winner, taking the ball between his thumb and two
fingers, proceeds with great dexterity, shuffling his hand

under the first, second, third and fourth moccasins, and
humming a ditty accompanied by some cabalistic words
invoking the aid of his patron deity. It now comes to the
opposing player to "find" at.the first, second, or third
"lift." If at the first, it counts a given number in his
favor,—say four; if at the second, two; and the third, one.
The latter player now takes the ball and goes through the
same process. Ten usually constitutes the game, but the
number is as the players may agree.

At this game a Wyandot and a Chippewa became
warmly engaged, betting lightly at first of the peltries
acquired during the winter's hunt. They had played an
hour or two each day for some days; the last loser, unwilling to yield the palm of victory, would insist upon a re-
newal of the contest. Thus day after day was spent. No
ulterior calls or demands were permitted to interfere with
or stay their maddened passion. Success vibrated between
the two with provoking uncertainty; still they played on.
The expostulations of their respective friends were fruitless. Pent up in a charmed circle which neither had the
moral force to break, they became devotees to this fatal
passion. At length luck began to favor the Wyandot;
beaver- and otter-skins began to accumulate upon the heap
of the latter. The Chippewa's pile began to "grow small
by degrees and beautifully less." The game was kept up.
At length the Chippewa's last pelt was gone; his rifle, in
a fit of desperation, was staked: that, too, was lost!

Here the protracted game must end; but fate had more
evils, yet undeveloped, to be brought upon the tapis—
their evil genius had more serious work on hand for them.
The Chippewa now offered to stake his life against the

8—

Wyandot's winnings. This was promptly refused. The Chippewa insisted, becoming frantic with rage, indignation and desperation, and obstinacy became fury. In thus parleying, the Chippewa used some offensive language to the Wyandot, who immediately accepted the challenge. They resumed their seats. The game went on; perspiration stood upon the forehead of the Chippewa. The last " lift " and " find " came to the Wyandot—a pause—a " lift "— a " find "!

" Lost! lost!! " frantically exclaimed the unfortunate Chippewa. Springing to his feet and uttering a yell, he bounded off in the direction of the fort, distant about a mile. The Wyandot, indignant at such an act of craven poltroonery, instantly pursued the fugitive. The latter, seeing his enemy in hot pursuit, redoubled his speed. Doubtful for some time seemed the race. The Wyandot began to slowly gain; shorter and shorter became the space between the pursuer and the fugitive. At length the latter, finding escape hopeless, halted and faced about, when the avenger laid his victim at his feet by plunging his knife deep into his heart.

Here was trouble. Hitherto the most amicable relations had existed between the two tribes. The Wyandot sachem ordered the arrest and confinement of the murderer till an accommodation could be effected with the exasperated Chippewas. The chiefs of the parties met in council; a formal demand was made for the murderer; this was declined. A bonus was offered, but it was rejected; other offers were made, but to no purpose. The mediation of the commanding officer was invoked; he promptly appeared and harangued the Chippewas with eloquence and power in the name of their good father the king, and offered in the character of peacemaker an additional bonus in goods out of the king's storehouse. This intervention met with no better success.

Now the prisoner arose and addressed the assembly; first, the Wyandots, requesting them to cease all further efforts in his behalf. Then turning to the Chippewas, he made a full statement of what had occurred between him and his friend, declaring that he had no intention of harming him had he stood up like a *brave,* nor did he intend to retain his rifle, knowing it was the means of his subsistence. *"But I slew him for his cowardice."* He then asked to be permitted to attend the funeral unmolested, pledging himself to return and surrender himself up. This was agreed to, but his liberty was to extend no farther than the close of the funeral.

The prisoner, being released on his parole, returned home, dressed and painted himself in such manner as to appear in the character of a mourner, and armed himself with tomahawk and scalping-knife. Thus equipped, he proceeded to the Chippewa encampment, and deliberately seated himself at the head of the corpse. The crowd in attendance were astonished at the display of impudence and audacity of the man. He expected to be immolated at the burial, and had hinted to some of his friends that some more Chippewas would bear him company. Everything being ready, the funeral party set out, the Wyandot walking near the corpse. Arriving at the grave, heedless of their suppressed threats and angry scowls he seated himself near the corpse. The burial over, he arose to his feet. A pause, as if awaiting some movement or signal, when an aged woman, weeping bitterly, approached the Wyandot and addressed him: " Wyandot, under that pile of earth lies my only son, who alone was my dependence and support. He is your victim. Your life is in my hands, but I thirst not for your blood. I have no one to look to for the support of myself and these fatherless and motherless children. My pathway is now dark and gloomy. I know not what to do now. Will you take his place—be my son, and a father to these children ? "

The answer was: " Woman of the Chippewas, I have heard your talk. My heart was hard, but your talk, and the tears of yourself and these children, have made it soft. Till now I knew nothing of the family and relatives of him I slew. *I will do it.* I will protect and support you and these orphans. I will be a son to you and a father to them. But," turning to the gathered warriors, " remember, I do this not because I fear your vengeance; no, but because I believe the Mighty Ruler requires this atonement at my hands."

Taking him by the hand, she added: " Now the spirit of my son will depart in peace to the beautiful hunting-grounds prepared by the Manitou for his Red Children."

Waving her hand to the crowd of scowling warriors, they slowly and sullenly dispersed.

The Wyandot made good his promise. He lived to bury his adopted mother. He was as a father to the children.

ANNOUNCEMENT.

The publication of the larger work on this subject by the author will follow. It is hoped that it will be in press in a short time. It is completed. It contains all the folklore of the Wyandots that is in existence, a full description of the Clan System and Government of the ancient Wyandots, with all the Wyandot names and terms. It will contain a very extensive vocabulary of the Wyandot language—the only one of any worth in existence; also a study of the language, with cuts of first attempts to reduce it to a written form. It will contain also the old Methodist hymns translated into the Wyandot tongue. In the way of history it will contain the important unpublished writings of Governor William Walker and Peter D. Clarke, the two native writers.

This is the only work ever attempted which deals in a thorough and systematic way with these subjects in a manner to be of any use to science. But it will not be a dry and scientific work. Those competent to judge have examined the manuscript, and pronounce it a book full of interest for the general reader. The late Professor Daniel G. Brinton, of the University of Pennsylvania, and one of the foremost American writers on these subjects, examined the manuscript, and gave it his unqualified approval.